Belle´s Story

ISBN: 978-1-945929-30-4

Cumberland Presbyterian Church

Text font: Verdana 12

FOREWORD

This is a biography: the life story of someone you probably never heard of, in one sense, an "illustrious nobody", but a person whose life touched and made a difference, abeit often unrecognized, in the lives of many others.

It is written as a novel but is neither completely fiction nor the whole story: just glimpses. Others may have facets of their truth that are part of Belle's story, but this, my small part, is true to the telling and the seeing as I remember it.

May there be blessings on all grandparents who take the time to share their life stories with their grandchildren.

Beginnings

Elizabeth Johnson (originally Johnston) was a potato-famine Scotts-Irish immigrant. Her Jacobite forefathers had fled across the channel after taking part in the failed attempt in 1745-46 to place "Bonnie Prince Charlie" on the throne of England. They took with them a ship load of trunks and crates with the fancy clothes, artfully woven bed hangings, and all the table settings deemed necessary for decent living.

In France they had lived for almost three decades in relative comfort despite dwindling resources, until the Revolution proclaimed them aristocrats and forced them to hurriedly pack a few family heirlooms and flee to Scots-Irish relatives in North Ireland. There the family slowly declined into genteel poverty, reduced to scrabbling a living from the rocky soil. Despite their present condition, they remembered former times of wealth and "polite society" by naming their daughter after their illustrious ancestor Elizabeth Fairfield: the same Elizabeth whose remaining wine glasses with the famous Jacobean thistle pattern still graced the mantle.

But when blight ruined the potato crop in 1845, hunger drove the Johnston family to America.

Too bad ship berths were so expensive that the family could only afford to bring the three younger children! The two older boys, being of an age to fend for themselves, had to be left behind in County Antrim and contact with them was eventually lost.

The crossing was rough and all on board suffered, but the ship made it through with most, but not all, of its passengers. Elizabeth's baby sister died as they came within sight of land and was buried the next day in New Orleans. Overland by cart the family went, thistle-engraved wine glasses and all, to - where else? - Johnstown, Pennsylvania. There young Elizabeth's pretty face and Irish brogue soon captivated Thomas Jefferson Adams, reportedly a descendant of John Adams and Abigail Smith.

Thomas Jefferson and Abigail: American names to add to the family heritage of Jacobite Elizabeth and Irish Adelia.

Since neither Thomas nor Elizabeth wanted to take sides in the mounting strife that was hurtling the country toward Civil War, they moved their growing family and the remaining Fairfield wine glasses to a farm in the frontier region of southwest Illinois where in 1888 Belva Lockwood was born, the last of ten living children with three others dead at childbirth or in first infancy.

Perhaps if there had been good doctors in the region Elizabeth's cancer might have been diagnosed earlier but, then again, what could have been done at that time? This last pregnancy proved too much: she never nursed the baby and was dead within six months.

Who would have thought raising a baby would be so much trouble? After all, there were enough daughters and daughters-in-law to take on that job, and all had experience in bottle-feeding the runts that every litter of pigs seemed to produce. But there was the catch: Belva (called Belle) wouldn't, couldn't tolerate the high-quality milk that provided the butter and cream on which the farm's economy was based. Not even milk from Thomas' highly-regarded brood mares was acceptable. Finally a cow was found several farms away: a runty cow whose low-fat milk, despite being disgracefully blue, made the baby thrive.

Thomas bought the cow without hesitation and Belva Lockwood lived to join siblings Florence Adelia, William Thomas, Ella Abigail, Fredrick Carl, Clarence Everett, Emma, Frank, Ruben Homer, and Minnie Mabel.

Country school

Is it true that *två tid fyra är åtta*?

In the late 1800's in what is now Mercer county, Illinois, local custom mandated classes be taught in the predominant language of the area. The Adam's farm was southeast of Viola in what is now called Rivoli Township where there seems to have been a large number of Swedish immigrants (a town named Swedona is a few miles north). So, through the four grades the school offered Belle Adams walked a short ways down the road to the one-room country school where this English-speaking Irish-heritage girl learned her first numbers and letters in Swedish!

While a person can learn to read, write, speak and understand quite well in another language, childhood prayers and basic arithmetic - especially multiplication tables - are almost always done in the language in which they were first learned.

All throughout her life Belle counted, "en, två, tre, fyra, fem, sex, sju, åtta, nio, tio" etc.

So, is it true that två tid fyra är åtta?

Puppy

Belle was very fond of the small dog of her childhood and youth: the years she spent on the farm in west Illinois before 1905. Despite the fact that the dog was regarded as a hard-working contributor to the well-being of the farm, it never had a name - just "Puppy".

Thomas Adams produced and sold top-grade cream and butter from a small, select herd of cows, and Puppy always helped bring the cows in for the afternoon milking, usually running just back of them barking to hurry them down the track. At some point he had learned to move a slowpoke along by grabbing on to the tip of her tail. Well, cows kick forward and a bit sideways to protect their udders, but horses kick straight back and Puppy's tail-hanging days ended the day he confused a horse with a cow!

He survived, and despite that mishap still considered himself in charge of the herd.

That was a real plus for the farm when an unexpected early-winter blizzard came through late one morning. Usually the cows stayed in the pastures until the first real stick-to-the-ground snowfall came, and then they were moved into the barn until spring. But with no TV weather channel or storm-warning radio, this blizzard came barreling down out of Canada and caught the region unprepared.

As soon as the storm started, Belle's father headed out to get the cows, but after a few yards he quickly saw the danger of being caught in the *white out*; he barely made it back to the house.

The next morning the storm had moved on, so Thomas strapped on snowshoes and started through the pastures looking for his herd with light-weight Puppy bounding beside him over the snow drifts. They searched for hours but not one cow was to be found anywhere and Thomas was about to give up, figuring his herd had laid down and frozen to death in the storm, when he heard Puppy barking frantically beside a haystack.

At that time hay wasn't baled but was stored loose. Part was hauled to the loft of the barn for use in winter and the rest was piled up in the pastures in six to seven foot stacks wrapped around a pole so the animals could get to the fodder throughout the fall. Now only the very top of the stack showed as a rounded mound of snow and there Puppy was barking and barking. Thomas plodded over, and after pulling away the snow and top layers of hay found his precious milk cows safe under the stack which had protected them from the storm. After a lot of shoveling and cajoling, he and Puppy managed to get the cows safely to the barn for the rest of the winter.

The Smoke House

Puppy saved the cows that day as he had saved Thomas the year before.

The first light freeze in early fall was the signal to slaughter the pigs raised for the family's yearly meat. Some of the minor parts of the meat was preserved in ceramic crocks sealed with lard and kept cold through the winter in the root cellar under the house, but the sausages and the major cuts of pork were treated in a small, tightly-built smoke-house where the smoke from a slow fire, fed with special woods and additives, cured and flavored the sausages, hams and sides of bacon. The cold weather insured sufficient time for the smoking process to take effect without the meat spoiling.

But, of course, that fire in the smoke house had to be tended to. Early one afternoon Thomas went in to add fuel but was careless when propping the door open: the stick he used was weakened and broke under the weight of the door, which was built to always swing shut and guarantee a close seal. When the door slammed shut, the wooden bar on the outside that secured it against "critters" fell and locked into place in its slot. Thomas was trapped, too far away for his daughter in the farmhouse on the other side of the barn to hear his shouts.

As he slowly smothered to death in a smoke-filled building just big enough for him to stand with his feet beside the slow-burning embers and his head in the hams, he realized Belle wouldn't miss him for another four or five hours! He could easily have died there if Puppy hadn't been a really smart dog. Sensing that Thomas was in trouble, instead of barking like crazy beside the smoke-house like most dogs, Puppy dashed all the way around the big barn, across the cobbled stable-yard, past the house vegetable garden and the chicken pen, all the way up to the back door where he set up such a racket that Belle came out to see what was the matter. Barking and running forward, then barking and looking back, Puppy drew her to the smoke-house where she raised the bar to release her now "well cured" father.

Both of them realized how close Thomas had come to death and were grateful to the dog, but Belle, a down-to-earth farm girl, asked her father: "*Well, Pa, couldn't you have at least peed to put the fire out?*" Solemnly her father stated: "*That durned fire had me so dry I couldn't even dribble!*"

Indians!

So, when Puppy barked, Belle, working in the kitchen, listened. The farm in western Illinois was at that time right on the frontier and native Americans came through frequently. This had once been a prime hunting ground as witnessed by the former buffalo wallow on the stream down a bit from the farm house. As a child she often found stone arrowheads there.

Although these were not the "wild" Indians of TV and movies, and now had frequent contact with the white settlers, they were still semi-savage nomads always on the lookout for a handout or something to carry away: usually chickens or tools left lying around. Small groups of four or five men would show up silently at the kitchen door and gesture for a handout of food. The last of thirteen children, Belle kept house alone for her widower father after all the older siblings had left. From the time she was ten or eleven until she left the farm she was mostly alone in the house and, although none of the natives ever made an untoward gesture, their looks were enough to frighten a young girl.

In summer, the smell of the rancid bear grease they used to dress their hair warned Belle of their presence long before they got to the house. Then she'd hurry to beat on the piece of railroad iron hung beside the back door to call her father and the hired men in from where they were working in the fields. In winter, when just the two of them were on the farm with Thomas mostly working in the barn and around the house, Puppy would be there to sound the warning. Then her father could come to stand beside Belle until the group had received their hand-out and moved off the property.

The Spring House

The farm's economy depended mostly on cream and butter, although Thomas did breed a few fine horses that made major, if infrequent, contributions to the family finances. There were fewer than twenty cows in his herd but they were top producers.

As the milk came in it was left to "rest" on the cool back porch so that some of the top cream could be skimmed off, bottled and stowed in the spring house half-way down the hill toward the buffalo wallow. Then, if sweet butter was wanted, the milk was brought into the kitchen to be churned. But many people wanted butter with more taste so part of the milk had a small amount of sour cream added so it would separate and then be churned.

This was woman's work and Belle was an expert before she turned ten. She knew how to prepare the wooden churn; could hear just when the butter started forming; could scrape the butter from the sides, top and plunger when she was barely tall enough to see into the churn. There was a marble slab on a table on one side of the kitchen to work and salt the butter before it was stamped with the wooden molds her father had carved, molds that left a fancy decoration on each large patty. As she squared off each block of butter, Belle carefully packaged it in a piece of the parchment paper Thomas bought from the Sears catalogue before carrying the tray-full down to the spring house - one of Belle´s favorite places.

The family's spring house of dressed stone was built into the side of a hill where a natural spring poured out into a small creek. The water welled up out of the hillside into a rectangular holding pool neatly built of river rock. Above the main pool stone shelves were set into the walls.

The spring house was especially important in warm weather. Cans from the afternoon milking would be set up to their necks in the rectangular pool to keep a while. One whole lot of cream and butter could be set down in the constant coolness of the spring house in the afternoon and kept until Thomas finished the next day's early morning milking and could harness up the buggy to take his products to town.

On summer afternoons, the trip to the spring house provided an excuse for a short respite from the hot kitchen where the wood-burning stove was always lit.

And the rest of the milk after the churning? Buttermilk was always on hand for pancakes, biscuits and cakes. Some sweet milk was kept to drink, but a good part of the excess was for the hens, or the house-raised piglets - there was usually a box beside the wood stove with several runts to be carefully hand-raised since farm families rarely let anything go to waste.

Off to the Dance

Reins firmly in hand, Minnie Mabel kept the mare at a steady pace, hooves beating out a jaunty rhythm as she pulled the little two-wheeled buggy (or cart) towards Viola. Sitting beside her next oldest sister, Belle chattered excitedly about this, her first dance.

For weeks Belle had been preparing: all the flounces on her petticoats had been carefully starched and ironed to maximum fullness. Her teenager's slight waist was now fashionably nipped in with a corset, and she had even sewn rows and rows of tiny frills on the bodice of her corset cover to make up for a minor (and hopefully temporary) forgetfulness on nature's part. The impeccable white muslin of her summer dress was trimmed in tiny blue ribbons to match her eyes and the wide ribbon that held back her long blond curls worn loose.

Belle was only fifteen, still a year away from putting her hair up, but old enough to accompany her sister to a dance.

The buggy was small, old, and poorly sprung so the girls had their feet braced against the splash board as they jogged and bounced along. Under the seat was a small carpet bag with their hair brushes, nightgowns and a change of chemise since they would spend the night in town with a friend's family rather than return home through the dark countryside late at night.

They were driving straight into the afternoon sun but wide-brimmed hats protected their complexions. And there was a brisk breeze from the west to freshen the day. Too brisk! The mare cocked her tail and the wind overcame the intentions of the splash board! Both girls' white muslin was ruined.

This was a major disaster!

There was only time for a couple of dances in the spring before serious crop work set in for the summer, work that would continue until after the fall harvest. Then there would be few dances before the snow came. But the spring dances were the time to catch a young man's eye, so that fine weather and good roads could help Sunday afternoon courting along. Then perhaps the harvest dances might bring an announcement that would cause the women to lay aside their regular sewing and busy their fingers through the winter embroidering sheets, pillow cases, towels and napkins, hemming tablecloths and quilting coverlets that would grace a new bride's house.

Well, that was not to be thought of now. Just turn the mare around and go home!

Spinster

At what age does a marriageable girl turn into a spinster? Well, in Mercer County in the early 1900's it was sometime before twenty!

Belle had a beau. Had... After six months or so spent eyeing each other from a polite distance, they embarked on almost a year of serious courting that ended, not at the altar but at grave-side. Jack, Belle's beau, died a couple of weeks after an ordinary cold turned into pneumonia.

All that was left of her fiance was a gold locket holding a snippet of hair and the photo of a serious young man, plus a little black mourning brooch, the only jewelry deemed appropriate in her circumstances. The locket was pretty and shiny and unfortunately years later caught the eye of a thief who thought the brooch not worth stealing.

After the year of mourning considered "proper" (even for a husband that wasn't yet a husband), Belle returned to "courting society" to find herself over the hill! During the almost three years of the courting and mourning process the rest of her age group had all gotten married.

She stuck it out at home for a long year until she realized that everyone had now written her off, assigning her to the role of caretaker to her widower father to be followed by a lifetime of being an aunt, or waiting to marry and take over some widower´s household.

Well, that was Mercer County, but it definitely was not Chicago, a city where manufacturing and commerce mixed with jazz, gin and sin. Off Belle went to live with her much older sister 'Deal (not Adelia, and most certainly NOT Florence Adelia!), married to Ed, a first-generation

American of German parents, who had changed his last name to Grove, either because it was easier to spell, or pronounce, or whatever. Ed changed his name but certainly not his tastes: he loved stewed sausage on top of mashed potatoes and gloriously tart sauerkraut!

Chicago was a big change from the farm: very exciting and, at the same time, a bit scary! There were a great number of handsome buildings to admire and a seemingly endless number of streets to explore, some safe and others not so safe, but Belle was intent on discovering them all.

There were so many people, but not many overtly friendly. Even though she had lived in relative isolation on the farm, still, Belle missed the easy company of folks in small towns where everyone knew everybody else and could stop and take time for a friendly greeting.

Fortunately 'Deal's apartment was over a laundry run by a Chinese family who proved to be extremely open to friendship with a young lady who would take the time to overcome the barrier of their heavily accented English. The circumstances of Belle's swedish-language schooling had gifted her ear to hear through accents and soon they were sharing cups of a slightly bitter tea received in quarterly packages sent from China. In fact, when Belle admired their impossibly delicate porcelain cups, they immediately presented her with two, one to use in the apartment and the other for sharing in the house quarters of the laundry.

Exploring was wonderful, but to Belle one of the most exciting things about city life was the fact that there, unlike the farm, a woman might get paid for her work. Although 'Deal and Ed were kindness itself, it seemed desirable to look for a job.

At this time the garment industry in Chicago was the city's third major employer and the single largest source of employment for women. Here Sears, Roebuck & Company based its mail order business. Here Hart, Schaffner & Marx set up its big factory.

Here was a chance to get a real job that paid real money.

A couple of doors down from the apartment was a tailor's shop and there Belle found work as an apprentice, learning the craft for a very small stipend. She was fortunate to work for an independent tailor since in the large factories wages were not only low, but conditions notoriously bad - so bad, in fact, that in 1910 a strike involving thousands of workers in the garment factories effectively closed down the industry for most of the year.

Although she wasn't directly affected, the general atmosphere generated by the strike got on Belle's nerves and she jumped when an opportunity for a job in another area opened up.

Yellowstone

It was an offer too good for any unmarried twenty-two-year-old to pass up! Three months at Yellowstone Park! Even if it did mean waiting on tables. Anyway, the Chicago apartment was sweltering in summer: no wonder Ed and 'Deal took off for their cabin in the North Woods of Wisconsin every year. Well, while they were "roughing" it in their little rustic cabin by the lake, sleeping in bunk beds and getting their water by the bucketful from the pump outside the front door, Belle would be living an adventure, enjoying fresh mountain air and meeting new people every day at the renowned Old Faithful Inn.

When she signed up to work at the lodge, Belle had been told she would need a practical black skirt and several simple white blouses for work; aprons would be supplied. But, because the waitresses and chambermaids were expected to mingle socially with the guests, she was advised to bring several outfits appropriate for afternoon tea, ice cream socials and early-evening get-togethers, but not formal dances. Belle was happy the full skirts and multiple petticoats of a few years ago had given way to simple, slightly gathered skirts falling straight from the waist to ankle length with only one light underskirt. Many young women had even abandoned corsets completely, but Belle always felt more comfortable with proper undergarments, even through the ones she now wore were lightweight and not designed to really cinch in her waist.

The tailor Belle worked for had advised her to buy the newly fashionable silks for her social dresses and stick to plain materials for her everyday work clothes and traveling outfit. 'Deal had been extremely generous with funds and even accompanied her on several shopping trips. With the material in hand and buttons found at Woolworths's store, Belle made up the outfits under the tailor´s guidance.

First of all she made two black gabardine skirts and four white poplin blouses, plus a nice brown summer-weight gabardine traveling outfit - skirt and fashionably long jacket with black frog fasteners and black cording on the sleeves to go with the black hat already in her closet. She planned to wear one of the white blouses to travel.

Then she set her hand to working with silk for the very first time. From a large piece of heavy-weight silk in a light teal color she made a loose, square-necked blouse with three quarter sleeves, and a very slim skirt that looked a bit like the hobble skirts that were just coming into fashion. But this skirt did not restrict her movements at all because the tailor showed her how to set in a series of pleats in back that gave the overall impression of a tight skirt but at the same time permitted comfortable walking.

Belle´s favorite, however, was the off-white light silk skirt with tiny vertical mauve and navy blue pin stripes. When matched with a loose blouse in similar but plain off-white silk, it made a spectacular outfit. She loved it so much that she had splurged on a length of silk in a matching mauve to make a long sleeved, open front tunic-like top which transformed it from an afternoon outfit into one that could be worn for evening social occasions. Inspired by the success of that outfit she went back and bought a length of simple black silk and made another open tunic top trimmed with pieces left over from the teal outfit. After one more blouse, white with a pattern of tiny black bows, to dress up a black skirt she felt confident she could mix and match to maximum effect for the months she would be at the park.

But as she began to put the clothes in her suitcase, Belle realized she had planned her wardrobe with Chicago's hot summer in mind: Yellowstone would be appreciably cooler. 'Deal was much taller and larger so she couldn't borrow anything from her. However her sister-in-law, Ruben Homer's wife Pearl, was much more her size and agreed to lend Belle a short black jacket that was obviously several years old and now slightly out of fashion. But its very simplicity, with tuxedo lapels and a waistcoat cut at the bottom, gave it a timeless look. The jacket, and a beautiful Chinese embroidered silk shawl the neighbors downstairs had given her would be sufficient to face any temperature changes.

Belle and the Bear

The job was everything Belle had imagined: the work wasn't that hard; the people were endlessly exciting; and the social life was a single girl's dream! The young waitresses were allowed, in fact, encouraged to add their youthful good looks and energy to any and all afternoon and early evening social events while off-duty.

The only drawback was the lack of indoor "facilities" available to the hired help. While the guest rooms had access to indoor plumbing, the employees' quarters were much more spartan.

Thinking of 'Deal and Ed and the outhouse back of their summer cottage in Wisconsin, Belle hurried down the trail back of the kitchens. A few yards away the new moon revealed the dim figure of a large gentleman returning from the battery of outhouses just beyond the little wooden bridge that spanned a small stream. It was embarrassing meeting someone knowing the errand that made each of them take that path; and as luck would have it, they'd have to pass each other just in the middle of that bridge! But she really had to use the outhouse, so Belle ducked her head and quickened her step.

She'd barely set her foot on the first log of the bridge when suddenly the figure doubled in height and let out an awful roar that made her raise her head just in time to see an enormous bear on its hind legs in the middle of the bridge, all its big, sharp teeth glinting in the moonlight!

Belle screeched, hiked her skirts and ran as only a country girl can run back to the safety of the kitchen! As she told and re-told her adventure, her heart stopped racing and her breathing calmed. Finally another waitress asked her if she'd feel safer if a couple of friends went with her on the trip back to the outhouse.

> *"Thanks, but I don't feel the need to go back right now - I guess that bear just scared it right out of me!"*

Wife

The trip to Yellowstone seemed to have opened up a new outlook on life for Belle. Back in Chicago she found time to make friends and have a social life because on December 5, 1914, David Johnson, a minister of the Gospel, performed the ceremony to marry Belva L. Adams - spinster, 26 years old and originally from Mercer County, Illinois, to Monta Ward Gist - bachelor, 31, originally from Leavenworth, Kansas.

Monta enjoyed a good job as manager of one of the many Woolworth stores in Chicago so Belle could once again focus on managing a household, but this time just for the two of them.

As was to be hoped, in the second year of their marriage Belle was expecting a child. Things went along normally until the time for delivery.

In Rivoli Township in 1888 Thomas Adams had no way of knowing that the opening between the two sides of Belle's heart had failed to close completely after birth: Belle was simply a baby that "failed to thrive". But once in Chicago doctors with stethoscopes were available and when her extreme fatigue in labor make it almost impossible to give birth, Belle's heart defect was finally diagnosed.

The doctor was skilled and the baby girl finally born and eventually christened Dixie. But the doctor's warning was stern: "*Her heart won't withstand another childbirth.*" What a fine husband she had! Monta promised there would be no more children and there weren't. But Belle's faithful husband was always there beside her.

Chicago's South Side

In the early 1920's, even near enough to downtown to hear the trains on the Loop, the streets of Chicago's south side were often mean. And a young neighborhood tough looking to make life miserable for graderschoolers walking home alone made them even meaner.

In those days children - even first graders - were taught - and expected - to walk to and from to school, even crossing busy streets. But every day on the way home from school this particular bully lay in wait for Belle's little daughter.

After several weeks of having Dixie come home with hair pulled, supplies stolen, and books thrown into the gutter, Belle was at a loss for a solution. But Monta, used to the ways of a big city, came up with this advice: "*Don't run, honey; just defend yourself with whatever you have in your hands.*"

That bully was very, very, sorry that little Dixie had been roller-skating that day. He never bothered her again.

Homesteaders

But something was wrong. Monta's health was slowly declining despite all the care she took of him. Finally the doctors told Belle that her husband would be dead in six months if he didn't get away from Illinois' cold weather. Their diagnosis: tuberculosis of the glands. Had the Army doctors known or guessed when they exempted Monta from service during the Great War? If so, nothing was mentioned at the time. But now his deteriorating health had become alarmingly apparent.

Treatment? In 1922 the only treatment available was to move to a warmer climate and pray.

Not one to spend time worrying, Belle immediately set about packing up the family things while Monta resigned as manager of the Woolworth store, and off they went with their little daughter on the train to homestead a section of undeveloped land near Frostproof, Florida.

Their intention was to take advantage of a law that provided for the transfer of up to 160 acres of unoccupied public land to each homesteading family on payment of only pennies per acre, on the condition they had lived on the land for five years and produced some sort of crop. If the family wished to buy the land after only six months of residence they could do so but at a much higher rate.

Florida wasn't an easy place to settle. A lot of the open ground between stands of trees in central Florida was (and still is) prime land for saw-palmetto, a vicious shoulder-high palm shrub that grows in clumps, some more than 20 feet in diameter: hundreds of acres thickly covered by pigmy palms whose circular-shaped leaves are deeply divided into many dagger-shaped segments stiffly held on saw-toothed stems some two to three feet long. Note the use of words such as "dagger" and "saw-tooth". Palmetto is not much good for anything except roasting hot-dogs: just hack off the saw-edges, skewer the hot-dog and hold over the fire: the stem doesn't burn.

But mostly palmetto is just plain nasty and almost impossible to get through, takes a backhoe and lots of work to grub out properly, and is filled with unpleasant "critters" such as snakes, red widow spiders, skunks, and humongous roaches.

As homesteaders Belle and Monta cleared patches of ground to plant vegetables, but every post hole dug immediately became a miniature pond due to the high water-table at that time. Fence posts rotted out in less than two years.

And then there were the "critters." Belle lived in fear that her little daughter playing outside around the house would meet up with an alligator trekking to a better water hole or off to visit a girl friend, or become entranced with one of the bright-colored Coral snakes that look so pretty and inviting to little hands. Not to mention the danger from other local venomous snakes: Copperheads, Water Moccasins, Diamondbacks, Canebrake rattlers and Pigmy (or woods) rattlers. And that Red Widow spider that likes to live in the palmetto has three other cousins, Southern Black, Northern Black, and Brown, who share parts of the state with the Brown Recluse Spider - all venomous. Of course, there were scorpions, too.

The farm back in Illinois never had so many dangerous neighbors, Belle thought - only Indians now and then.

Besides all that, there were (and still are) ticks, sand fleas, and chiggers (red bugs) to be dealt with! (Fire ants are fun, too, but they came later!)

It's not that Monta and Belle picked the wrong part of the state to settle in; south Florida has its own charming vegetation: saw-grass, the plant that inspired the phrase 'river of grass' for the Florida Everglades. Imagine trying to wade through thick clumps of grass with blades that grow up to nine feet long, each equipped with sharp little saw teeth along both edges as well as down the underside of the midvein! Saw-grass can rip clothing and skin to shreds in no time. And saw-grass means more "critters," mostly alligators in large numbers.

A high water-table and frequent hurricanes meant dealing with those alligators, lots of snakes, and other animals driven from their swampy lairs onto higher ground - often "people places," that is, houses and barns - looking for a safe spot to wait out the storm.

The family had barely settled on their chosen plot of land when a telegram arrived urging Belle to return to the farm to say good-by to her dying father. On that long, sorrowful train trip home Belle had plenty of time to ponder the hows and whys that brought her to this point. She knew her family - indeed, society in general - expected her, as the youngest daughter, to remain home to take care of her father, eventually filling the role of a permanent spinster aunt.

She was sorry that Thomas had been forced to hire a neighbor woman to come in three times a week to "see to" the house and prepare food so he could have a hot noon meal every other day (either heating up or eating cold food the rest of the time). She was sorry her sister had needed to leave her own family in order to hurry to her father's bedside those last few days. Yes, she was sorry for all that, but not at all sorry she had chosen to leave home, marry and have a family of her own.

The trip was long and the train seemed extremely slow; she barely arrived in time for the funeral. Almost everything desirable had been divided up among the sisters when their mother died, so it only took a couple of days to go through what was left before the farm was sold with its furnishings, animals, and tools.

As she sorted through years of memories, Belle found four dusty wine glasses that seemed oddly out of place among the mail-order furnishings of the house. None of the sisters had wanted them: after all, there were only four and in no way fashionable. But after 'Deal told her what was known of their background, Belle carefully wrapped them up, and carried them back to the Florida homestead with her. But she never unpacked them there: they seemed out of place in such a setting.

The little family never acquired their homestead: they left before the residency requirement was fulfilled. The rigors of trying to grub out palmetto and farm the scrub land wore out both Belle and Monta, but most especially Monta, who was not farm-bred and whose health was precarious.

Belle, too, was at a disadvantage: she quickly realized that few of her Illinois-acquired farm skills applied to Florida. That first year she carefully planted her vegetables as she had in the north, in late spring. Barely had the plants taken root when the blaze of the summer sun withered them completely. How was she to know that vegetables had to be planted so much earlier in Florida? Even the moon lore learned at home seemed not to work this far south. Every month Belle would scan the evening sky to see if the new moon showed as a bowl holding the water that promised a "wet" month, or was tipped on its side having spilled out its water, thus signalling a "dry" month. But in Florida the rains didn't seemed to pay any mind whatsoever to the moon.

So by 1925, much to Belle's relief, the family had given up homesteading and moved some 30 miles to "civilized" Bartow where Monta found a position managing a filling station and Belle set up household in a small, run-down rental cottage on the edge of town. That house was filthy! So dirty in fact, that there was no way to wash it clean. So before moving in, Belle whitewashed the entire house inside and out, room by room from top to bottom, walls and ceilings, and then scrubbed the floor on her hands and knees, saying she could live poor but absolutely couldn't live in dirt.

Monta´s solution

"Your daughter is developing a curvature of the spine", the doctor warned. *"If you want her to grow up properly, she'll need to wear a full body brace through adolescence."*

The doctor's diagnosis was very worrisome to Belle, but the very thought of this free-ranging eleven-year-old laced into a restrictive corset set Monta's teeth on edge. He'd fostered a spirit of independence by allowing his daughter a great deal of personal freedom. Typically, when Belle protested loudly that their Dixie was going to wind up getting bitten by a snake if she kept roaming the palmetto flats, Monta hadn't forbidden the forays into the wild: just bought her a rifle and taught her how to shoot. So he just couldn't see his way to start reining her in now. *"Don't worry, doctor. I can take care of it."*

It only took a day for Monta to set up a trapeze in the yard. In less than a week his daughter had mastered the basics and was eagerly looking forward to more active exercises. Several years of constant work on the trapeze not only straightened her spine but also developed a healthy, athletic girl with exceptionally strong back and shoulder muscles.

Mr. Bartow Smith

1929 wasn't a good year to begin with: annual income was down to $750 for those living in industrial areas; for farm people, it was only $273. The year ended worse: the stock market started its crash on October 24, reaching catastrophic levels on "Black Tuesday," October 29. Rumors ran rife around the country and when panic set in people began massive withdrawals from banks causing one bank after another to fail in 1930.

At thirteen Belle felt her daughter was old enough to go shopping by herself in Bartow. She sent her with a dollar bill to buy a remnant of yard goods for 21¢. The change came, of course, in coins. As Dixie left the store she saw a large number of people trying to get into the bank down the street to withdraw money and it was obvious they were not getting satisfaction. She immediately turned around, re-entered the store and asked if she could return the cloth. They gave her money back in coins.

One result of the bank failures was that people no longer accepted paper money, insisting instead on "real" money: coins that carried their value in the actual metal they were stamped from.

The family lived for over a month on that dollar in coins. But eventually even that ran out.

And then along came Mr. Bartow Smith (the one who bought the Cunningham house), well-known as a true Southern gentleman. He showed up at the back door holding a basket with over a dozen eggs. With great courtesy he explained to Belle in his Southern drawl that his *"hens had laid too many eggs for them to hatch and would she please do him the favor of taking these eggs off his hands and hatching them out.¨* !!!!

Farm girl Belle knew just what to do and soon had a nice flock of laying hens. But those eggs were never laid by ordinary farm-yard chickens: they were store bought, guaranteed to produce sturdy chicks: chicks that developed into top-quality Plymouth Rock hens with their characteristic black and white stippling.

Mr. Smith claimed he could never understand how his hens had gotten their eggs "all mixed up," and when Belle tried to share the chickens or the eggs they laid, he refused, noting that she had done all the work of hatching and raising those chickens; he hadn't even had to lay the eggs!

In a world without paper money, barter soon became a way of life. Belle's farm-girl skills came in very handy: those chickens and the eggs they produced kept the family in food and clothing throughout the Great Depression and a few years later sent Dixie to college.

Purdue

Belle had a fourth-grade education, the highest grade taught in the country school down the road from the farm where she grew up. Monta had a high school degree and enjoyed reading, especially classical English literature. He even owned a complete set of Shakespeare's plays, each volume beautifully bound in red leather with the title in gilt. He encouraged his daughter to read: her childhood books included one on Greek mythology, a copy of Well's *Outline of History* and the King James' Bible with front and back covers of olive wood from the Holy Land, a gift from her father. (The inscription inside shows that he had beautiful penmanship.)

But when Dixie graduated from high school in 1934 she was at loose ends as to what to do with her life. A friend encouraged her to enter the Miss Florida pageant which in those days did not mean parading around in a swimsuit: preliminary judging of entries was done from studio portraits. (No doubt the swimsuits would come later.) The idea of competing for a title that could take her to the Miss America 1935 pageant was exciting and she submitted her photos.

Belle and Monta hit the roof and forced her to withdraw her name, even though she had been selected as one of the finalists. They wanted more for their daughter and felt education, not beauty pagents, was the key to a better life. But the country was still reeling from the Depression and Monta's job as manager of a filling station had been affected by the economic slow-down, so how the family could afford to send her to college is beyond understanding. But college it was to be.

Once the decision was made, the choice of Purdue University was quite logical: the university had called Amelia Earhart to serve on the faculty as *Counselor in Careers for Women* and *Adviser in Aeronautics*. Like many young women of her day, Dixie was in love with adventure, and the greatest adventure of her time was airplanes. It took a year to arrange a scholarship for the exceedingly bright young woman graduating at the head of her class, even if it was from some out-of-the-way school in Florida. But a scholarship doesn't pay for clothes.

The family couldn't afford a sewing machine, but Belle got out her needle and thimble from her years as a tailor's apprentice in Chicago, raided her egg-money savings to buy yard-goods, and spent months making her daughter's college clothes: three suits, four day dresses, a coat, two waltz-length party dresses and two full length evening dresses! All by hand!

Those clothes, along with her good looks and easy familiarity with classical literature, were enough to get Dixie into a good sorority and open doors to social functions designed to put beautiful, well-bred young ladies into the company of refined, well-educated bachelors with a future. 1935 was Big Band era and Dixie danced almost every weekend to Glen Miller and Tommy Dorsey, mostly in the Chicago area: her dance cards were all full. On two evening dresses! Actually it seems all the sorority sisters engaged in massive lending and borrowing of clothes, plus a great deal of adding and removing flounces, flourishes, and ornaments so as not to appear to be wearing the same evening dress over and over (as if men would ever notice the difference!)

Things seemed to be going along quite well despite a straight "C" average - due, no doubt, to an excess of social life, when suddenly Dixie's world unraveled. In 1937 Monta Ward's illness worsened to a point where he could only work part time and so less and less money came in to pay expenses at Purdue.

A letter from Belle called her daughter, still single, home at the end of her sophomore year.

A couple of months later, while attempting to fly around the world at equator-level, Dixie's heroine Amelia Earhart left New Guinea and disappeared into myth.

Jeff

Soon after returning to Bartow Dixie found a beau. Jeff Gentry always seemed to Belle to have a wild streak that may or may not have run in his family. Supposedly all the Gentrys in the United States are related somehow through one Nicholas Gentry who came from England in the late 1600's to settle in Virginia. There are lots and lots of branches to the family but Jeff apparently descended from some who settled in the Kentucky foothills of Appalachia at the end of the 1700's. A generation or two later, the arrival of a new baby year after year in an area not known for wealth provided a huge incentive for two of the oldest boys, Richard and William, to leave home before the age of sixteen. Westward they went in search of fame and fortune.

William soon disappears from our story, but there on the frontier, living among a group of Native Americans in southern Oklahoma, Richard Gentry found more than fortune: he found a wife, whether Kiowa, Osage or Comanche is unknown, in any case, an Native American wife.

Lisbet was her name. Not Elizabeth nor even Betty - just Lisbet. The story is he "stole" her. But that probably doesn't mean he carried her off kicking and screaming; more likely he was kind, not bad looking, and seemed to offer some sort of future. In any case they left her people and started life as a couple.

It seems things went along pretty well until Lisbet became pregnant. As the months went by she became more and more despondent until finally the whole story was coaxed out of her one word at a time in halting English: she was unhappy because she didn't consider herself properly married. He hadn't paid for her!

The Kentucky boy proved his love: he loaded up a couple of mustangs with salt, flour and sugar, a hunting rifle and munitions (and most likely a small keg of liquor, too), took them off to Lisbet's brother who was now the head of the family, and so bought his wife properly, thus establishing her position as a married woman according to tribal custom.

As far as is known, they had only one child, who they named Jefferson Richard and raised in or near Corsicana, Texas. Eventually Lisbet was left a widow - a rich widow, a rich Indian - which apparently didn't sit too well with her white neighbors. But there was little they could do as money in large quantities is a great incentive for tolerance and the observance of social courtesies.

Despite rejection as a "half-breed," with the help of the family's money Lisbet's son finally found a wife named

Mary Martin. Jefferson and Mary had two sons, Jefferson Richard, Jr. (born 1905) and William (born 1907), who lost their mother sometime before 1910 to an unknown illness, and their father in 1920, one of the last victims of the Spanish flu. The orphaned boys were sent to stay with distant relatives in Bartow, Florida, and most of their family mementos, papers, and inheritance were lost in the move.

How much of the story is true? No way to tell. There are just too many undocumented events. But that was the story Jeff told and accompanied with the photo of a stern, dark, moon-faced old lady dressed up to her chin in abundant Victorian black - Lisbet, he claimed.

And it could well be true. In any case, Jeff's slightly swarthy good looks and "bedroom eyes" entranced the girl who had danced to Tommy Dorsey's band in Chicago and now sulked in resentment at being forced to finish her education at a podunk college in Florida's panhandle. Dixie had stuck it out at *Florida Female Seminary* in Tallahassee for only a year before returning to her little hometown in mid-state with no vision for her future.

Yes, Jeff was handsome and, despite the Depression, his car dealership was prosperous so he was always riding around town in the hottest, latest model Ford just out of Detroit. Money and looks soon led to an engagement.

Belle wasn't at all happy about the relationship: Jeff was divorced. In fact, he and his former wife Mildred had married and divorced three times! When asked, Mildred simply said he was "hard to get along with."

Dixie married Jeff on September 16, 1939, and soon Belle found out what Mildred had meant. Her son-in-law had a short fuse - extremely short, and her daughter was very used to getting her own way.

So the two of them embarked on a series of cat-and-dog fights that were a scandal throughout the town. Between fights they lived a fast-paced social life: dances, dining out, weekend trips to Cuba for night clubbing and gambling, fine riding horses, new cars, and stylish clothes.

But the good times were always punctuated by scenes that ended in dish-throwing or black eyes.

No wonder after less than three years Dixie was looking for a way out of her miserable situation. But Belle just didn't have the time to sit and commiserate with her: Monta had taken a turn for the worse and could no longer work at all. Fortunately, despite his temper, Jeff also had a kind heart and a generous hand so rent money, food and medicines were never lacking.

Then, suddenly, Belle was bewilderingly, overbearingly, completely, alone. No sooner had Monta Ward died in the Lakeland hospital on February 15, 1943, than her daughter found a way to fulfill her thirst for adventure that at the same time enabled her to leave home with no condemnation from society: there was a war on and she was off to do her part!

WASP

"Yes, I know you have a civilian pilot's license, but what the Women's Airforce Service Pilots Corps really needs are mechanics."

"??? "

"Those planes come back from the war front in bad shape and have to be repaired before they can be flown in battle again. As soon as we know for sure they're fixed they get sent right back to the war. But thinking about it, somebody needs to take them up for a test flight before we sign off on them. And those Flying Fortresses are heavy: it takes a lot of muscle-power to pull them up. There's no men around for that and most of you girls are just too light-weight for the job. But you look a bit stronger than most. Care to give it a try?"

"!!!"

So, thanks to the muscles formed on the trapeze her father set up for her, Dixie Gist Gentry became a W.A.S.P., learned to put motors together but, most importantly, test-flew repaired P-51 fighters known as *Mustangs* and B-17 heavy bombers known as *Flying Fortresses*.

Thanksgiving Leave

Dixie was assigned to the W.A.S.P. base in Sweetwater, Texas, and, although her letters were full of news and photos of her fellow W.A.S.P.s, she showed no inclination to visit Florida for almost a year.

Then at Thanksgiving, authorities not only gave her leave but insisted she go home for two weeks' vacation. There must have been some sort of an understanding with Jeff, because a couple of months later she phoned Belle in tears with the news that she was pregnant.

As soon as her condition became obvious, the Air Corps informed her that she could no longer fly, and therefore was out of the program (that was due to end soon, anyway since the war would end that same year and the W.A.S.P Corps dissolved).

Dixie was not overly enthusiastic about the prospect of coming home to live, but did have the excitement of settling in to a new house. Of course, she wanted Belle with her to help her through her pregnancy.

Lakeland

Bartow was pretty much a small town in Jeff's eyes. At least Lakeland at that time had some "society," so Jeff bought a house there.

After living in small, dingy rental places, Belle thought this was a lovely house. It was newly built in Florida bungalow-style with full porches across the front and back plus a sun room down one side. A very large living room stretched along the whole front of the house to the sun room, with a fireplace on one end (that never managed to warm the long room on coolish nights), and an archway at the other end opening into the dining room that was the central traffic zone for the whole house. The sun room had French doors onto the dining room, the living room and the front porch, but usually all but the ones to the dining room were kept locked. The walls of the sun room were all glass but the big pine trees in the front and side yards kept it cool.

On the left of the dining room a hallway gave entrance to two bedrooms and the house's one bathroom. In the back wall a door led straight to an oversized kitchen with one end divided into a pantry, a breakfast nook and a short hallway to the screened back porch.

To make the nursery, the end of the porch off the main bedroom was closed in and a tiny closet built in one corner. The little room had two windows, a door into Dixie's room and a door onto the porch, so there was barely room for a crib.

Along the side of the house opposite the sun room was a porte-cochere: a roofed drive-though with steps directly to the front porch so as to be able to park and take things in without getting wet on the way to the garage itself, which was a separate building in back.

It was a relatively new neighborhood and the only immediate neighbors were an elderly couple, Mr. and Mrs. Brown, whose house was just beyond the porte-cochere. Since the lots on the opposite side and in back were undeveloped, they were overgrown with weeds, and full of field rats and snakes.

The road between Lakeland and Bartow was a narrow, winding two-lane black top. So, although his official residence was now in Lakeland, because the dealership closed late, and he did not want to drive that narrow, dangerous road at night, during the week Jeff stayed at a hotel in Bartow and came home on the weekends.

He said he felt it was OK to spend the week away since Belle had come stay with Dixie so she wouldn't be alone during her pregnancy.

Credit cards were not available at the time and although the bills were paid and the pantry always full, Jeff had a habit of forgetting to leave money in the house. About two weeks before her due date Dixie got anxious and told Belle feared she'd go into labor with no cash on hand. So early one morning she drove to Bartow, went straight to the hotel, and found Jeff had established a Monday-through-Friday relationship with a local girl.

Belle had heard rumors. In fact, what she'd been told is that when Jeff rode his beautiful Tennessee Walker horse in Bartow's 4th of July parade that year, one girl in her late teens had remarked to her sisters how handsome he looked. The older girls had already earned a reputation for wild behavior and dared their younger sister to "set her cap for him" and she took the dare.

Divorce

No matter who had seduced whom, it did not sit at all well with Dixie. She came home absolutely outraged. Belle understood but thought her rage a bit overdone. In any case Dixie banished Jeff from the house. Her daughter was born at the end of August and named Michele Adelia (for her great-aunt 'Deal). In less than a month Dixie had filed for divorce.

It didn't sit well with the court either because the Monday-through-Friday girl was a minor (in those days anyone under 21 was considered a minor) - not only a minor, a now-pregnant minor! The court not only admitted the suit for divorce but, in consideration of his "depraved" behavior, Jeff was forbidden all unsupervised visits with his daughter.

Jeff fought the divorce tooth and nail. For some reason he didn't want to be free from the marriage, but not from any scruples about divorce itself since he'd been down that road before. Belle heard a whisper around Bartow that he didn't want to be free to marry his Monday-through-Friday girl, which might just be true because in the almost four years they were together after the divorce was final, he never married her, although he lived with her and provided for his second daughter, born less than a year after the first.

The prolonged court battle was noisy, messy, and thoroughly mean-spirited on both sides. Apparently the scandal and court battle finally soured Jeff on life. He sold the dealership, set up a small loan business, and moved his new family far out of Bartow to an old renovated fishing shack on Eagle Lake, some eight miles down the road toward Lake Wales.

For her part, Dixie threw herself into enjoying life. As soon as the weather turned fine in the north she, Belle, and the baby took a six-month trip to see friends in Georgia and all the relatives in Chicago, Iowa, and Michigan. She also tried to embrace her love of adventure in ways Belle did not entirely approve of.

1947

"Very interesting resume. Plenty of hours in large planes. And I see your pilot's license is up to date. So, you say you're interested in our job offer of flying cargo to and in Colombia? Do you know where Colombia is?"

"____."

"OK. And are you aware the country has few navigational aids? Basically our pilots fly by sight, following the Magdalena River inland from the coast until changing course over the mountains to the capitol."

"____."

"OK. One final thing, the contract we use specifies that in the event a plane goes down, the company is not obliged to, nor will make any effort to search for the crew."

"!!!"

"Understood. Sorry you won't be joining our company. I understand perfectly that an infant daughter does change one's priorities in life. Thank you for coming in."

So instead of flying cargo planes in South America, there was an endless round of evening bridge games at Elliott's house, afternoon drives south to the Raulerson family home, and countless trips to the beauty salon in downtown Lakeland where Dixie would have her hair and nails done and chat with Edie (Edith) and Alice, two friends who did exhibition water-skiing at near-by Cypress Gardens.

But through all this Belle was getting tired of being an unpaid baby-sitter, tired of being treated worse than hired help. She was tired of being tied to the house with no time to visit with friends while Dixie went off to party and play bridge. Even though she had the car Jeff had given her during Monta's last illness, she rarely got out because Dixie was never home to take over the care of the baby. Most of all Belle was tired of her daughter's up-and-down moods and rough tongue. When a friend mentioned a job opening as a receptionist and switch-board operator at a tourist resort in New Port Richey over on the Gulf Coast, Belle jumped at the opportunity.

All her life, except for those few years in Chicago, Belle had been taking care of family members. Now with her husband gone, perhaps it was time for her to live her own life; time for her adult daughter to take her affairs in hand and stop depending so much on her mother.

True, she had only worked outside the home those few years so long ago in Chicago and Yellowstone Park, but Belle felt confident she could handle the job. The pay was only mediocre but the position came with food and housing and held the promise of freedom.

Belle so looked forward to a respite from the house in Lakeland, plus, since she thoroughly enjoyed meeting new people, this could be more fun than Yellowstone!

She took the job, leaving Dixie, the baby, and Phoebe in Lakeland.

Phoebe

Phoebe was very a misleading name because Phoebe was a boy: a large easy-going black tomcat with a girl's name! He had wandered in as a tiny stray at just the wrong age to tell "him" from "her" and so got a girl's name from Dixie, along with a bed Belle fixed for him on the back porch. That was a couple of weeks before Michele was born and the arrangement lasted until the day the baby arrived home from the hospital when he took over a corner of her room. Belle worried that the cat might try to sleep in the crib, but apparently he was happy just to be in the same room with the baby and never tried to get in beside her.

Phoebe was really the best of playmates: he never minded being dressed in doll's clothing (all the panties had holes cut to accommodate his tail), nor objected to being paraded around the house in Michele's little play stroller. She could chatter away to him by the hour or they would listen to records together: he never interrupted or got bored.

In the middle of the afternoon he would sit and share her snack. One of belle's best memories was watching Phoebe on a chair across from her granddaughter at the little play table on the back porch. The almost-three-year-old would carefully take a grain of her favorite puffed wheat from her bowl and put it in the middle of the table, and Phoebe would use one paw to gently pull it toward him to eat. Share and share alike: one for Michele, one for Phoebe; another for Michele, another for Phoebe.

Go figure how an all-black cat came to be named Phoebe, a name of Greek origin meaning "bright, radiant"! If the name had been a more common one, it might have been changed slightly when his gender became apparent, like Tommy into Thomasa or Tiger into Tiger Lily, but what can be done with Phoebe?

But where was Phoebe, Belle asked herself, the day the baby found the rat in her sandbox? And what was the rat doing in the sandbox? It must have been sick, or old, or starved since it submitted to the child's handling. The toddler must have thought it was hungry since, without saying anything to anyone, she went in the house and got some cheese to feed it. After all, in her little story books mice ate cheese, didn't they? No matter that this was huge ugly field rat, not a cute little story-book mouse. It was all the same to her. Touching was one thing, but trying to stuff cheese into its resisting mouth was more than the rat could stand: it bit!

It didn't just bite, it clamped its teeth all the way through the web of skin between the thumb and first finger of Michele's right hand, and then refused to let go! Needless to say, the child´s screams brought people from the house and from next door to kill and remove the rat. The corpse went to Animal Control while the baby was whisked off to the emergency room.

Considering that all the unbuilt lots in back of the house were shoulder-high with weeds, one field rat isn't so surprising. But when Belle heard about it she wondered what her granddaughter was doing outside unsupervised in the sand box? She wasn't quite three yet!

That back yard! It was only a few months later, just after her third birthday, that the child fell out of a orange tree she was trying to climb and was picked up screaming with a small stick jammed into her forehead. Belle heard it took three nurses to hold her granddaughter down so the emergency room doctor could inject enough anesthetic to clean the wound and close it with four stitches. Almost more nurses than stitches.

How proud little Michele was of those stitches when they finally came out! The nurse bribed her to sit still during the process with the promise of giving them to her, so home she went with a matchbox containing the precious little pieces of black thread. Belle was allowed to admire them a bit and then it was straight off to Mrs. Brown to share the treasure with her. Mrs. Brown's kitchen door was an open invitation to a little girl left to roam around and play outside with little or no supervision.

At the beginning of 1948 the Brown's grandson, Gabe, came from Israel with his parents for a couple of month's visit in America before returning to their home on a communal farm. Gabe was just about four, close to Michele's age, and spoke only Hebrew. Michele, of course, spoke only English, but Belle was amazed how well they got along, playing together on the front sidewalk and lawns all day, and with no problem at all communicating in some sort of mutually understood child's language.

Mimi

It was about that time that Belle's granddaughter got a new name. Right after Gabe and his parents returned to

Israel, Belle decided it would be good for Dixie to get out of Lakeland, away from the on-going conflict with Jeff. The hotel practically shut down during the hottest summer months so Belle asked for and got an unpaid leave of absence. Her sister 'Deal loaned them the cottage in Wisconsin for the summer, and so the family headed north.

The cottage was just a spartan, unheated wooden frame house with a wood burning stove and no running water nor indoor bathroom: there was a hand pump in front and an outhouse in back that no one was allowed to use after dark because of roaming bears. But the woods were delightfully cool and refreshing, and Belle enjoyed the simple life because it reminded her of her years on the farm in Illinois. The property was right on a lake with clear and icy water, although swimming was discouraged because the water was infested with leaches.

Most of the trades-people in the area were of Swedish extraction and not only spoke that language but also spoke English with a marked accent. That accent soon rubbed off on the child who seemed to have a good ear for language sounds. She had picked up lots of Yiddish from Mrs. Brown who spoke it with her husband (but not to her neighbors), some Hebrew from little Gabe, and in that summer she was beginning to sound very "Swedish." Belle laughed until tears came the day her granddaughter ran up the slope from the lake calling for her mother to complain in a heavy "Svede" accent: "*Mamma, O've a yeach on my yeg!*" (I've a leach on my leg.)

That same summer when 'Deal and Ed came to visit, German-extraction Ed began to call Michele *schnickelfritz*, an affectionate name for a lively, talkative child. She hated it! And retorted by saying, "*Me dis Mimi*": her way of asserting "I'm just me, not *schnickelfritz*." Belle thought the name was cute and it stuck, so Michele became Mimi, which everybody liked better than Mickey which Jeff used.

Maggie

The job at the tourist resort in New Port Richey was everything Belle had hoped for: there were plenty of tourists, mostly from the North, to greet and get to know; the other staff members were friendly; and the housing, actually the resort's smallest unit with one bedroom, a bath and a small sitting area, was adequately comfortable. Still very much a small town, downtown New Port Richey nevertheless had well-stocked businesses and there was the added attraction of a quiet walk along the Pithlachascotee River that ran right through the middle of town.

Manning the switch board had seemed a bit complicated at first. The resort had four incoming and multiple internal lines serving some 28 extensions. Each line was a cable that could be plugged into any one of the different extension receptors so residents could receive and make outside calls and also call the internal extensions. At peak times the connections to the different cabins and departments seemed as tangled as spaghetti, but Belle quickly mastered the board while serving as receptionist at the same time. She found the switch board so entrancing that she bought a toy replica with two lines and four receptors for her granddaughter.

But shortly after returning from Wisconsin a call from Mrs. Brown in Lakeland came through Belle's switchboard. Quite upset, Mrs. Brown explained that apparently Dixie would sometimes shut herself in her bedroom all day and forget she had a small daughter who got hungry -- a daughter who was smart enough to go to the neighbors and ask for lunch. Mrs. Brown didn't mind feeding Mimi, of course, but the situation worried her.

And, of course, the information worried Belle. But what was she to do? She couldn't let her granddaughter be neglected and neither did she want to return to Lakeland.

The solution was to hire Maggie, a slight Afro-American woman in her late 40's, a quiet, kind, strong woman married to "the Rev. John" who worked Monday through Saturday for the Lakeland Sanitation Department and on Sundays was the pastor of a thriving "free will" church in the African-American community near the hospital.

Belle didn't know it at the time, but as Dixie's depression worsened, Maggie would often take her charge home with her on the weekends where Mimi sat in the first row left of center with the pastor's family, the only blond head in the congregation.

But whatever it was Maggie did, it seemed to make her granddaughter thrive and the accidents stopped, so Belle was grateful.

The Sun Room

The sun room in the Lakeland house belonged to Mimi. She never played in her bedroom or any other place in the house except for snacks with Phoebe on the back porch.

Belle enjoyed seeing all her granddaughter's play-things carefully arranged: the dolls with their toy bath, the toy stroller and crib, a little table and chairs where she "worked" with crayons, scissors, paste and colored paper. Perhaps Jeff had only limited visitation rights, but he lavished toys and clothes on his daughter.

Mimi and Phoebe spent many hours there playing dolls (with Phoebe playing the part of the doll), or with Phoebe sleeping in the doll's crib while the child drew or made handcraft projects such as stringing beads. All down the long wall were bookshelves under the windows to hold supplies, books and records. Jeff had bought Mimi her own little record player, although after she turned four she was allowed to use the big one in the dining room.

Belle read to her a lot those first years and the child quickly learned to identify words and then read, but before she could read there were the Golden Books that came with an accompanying small record. How she liked to hear her granddaughter sing along to *Down by the station early in the morning* and chant with *The Little Train That Could*: "*I think I can, I think I can, I think I can, I know I can.*" Mimi had a good memory and knew all the words to every one of her records.

Dixie, too, liked music and had lots of records - the big 78 size. After little Mimi was allowed to use the big record player she played her mother's collection of 30's big band hits: *Tuxedo Junction, String of Pearls*, etc. Dixie had also collected a great deal of classical music and, although Belle personally didn't care for the operas - especially the German ones, she and her granddaughter enjoyed listening to Beethoven, Saint-Saëns, and even Rachmaninoff's crashing chords. Her granddaughter's favorite was Debussy's *The Sunken Cathedral*, but personally Belle preferred *The Carnival of the Animals*.

There were also a number of late 40's blues records and Mimi especially liked singing along at full volume to the chorus of one of Dixie's favorites, *Irene Good Night*:

Irene good night, Irene good night,
good night Irene, good night Irene,
I'll see you in my dreams.

But sometimes Belle wondered what the child made of the line *"Sometimes I have a great notion to jump in the river and drown."*

Crisis

Belle drove to Lakeland for Mimi's fifth birthday. But the child seemed strangely subdued. And she had bruises on her legs: apparently Dixie had used a orange tree switch on her. Yes, she was a hand-full: energetic, independent, full of curiosity, and prone to go where she wanted, when she wanted. Yes, she was often getting into things and not particularly obedient. But the bruises were not a good sign. And the child flinched at any raised voice.

Belle remembered the incident right after Christmas when her granddaughter had burned her hand on the little iron that came with a toy ironing board: Jeff's Christmas present. That toy iron heated up too much for a small child, but Maggie had shown Mimi how to press handkerchiefs with the understanding she was only to use the iron with Maggie present.

However one Saturday afternoon when Maggie was off, Mimi decided her doll's dress was wrinkled, set up the board and plugged in the little iron. She had seen Maggie test her iron many times with a spit-wet finger, but a child's reaction time is very slow and she had laid her whole hand on the iron!

What would most children have done when burned like that? Run screaming to mama!

Not Mimi.
Not to her mother.

When Belle arrived from New Port Richey she was alarmed to find the board set up and the iron tumbled on the floor. Dixie was in her room with the door shut so she went looking for her granddaughter and found her hiding in the back of her closet holding a very burnt hand and crying quietly. Mimi said she had hidden because she was afraid of getting yelled at. The whole situation worried Belle very, very, much but, outside of Maggie, she had no idea of how else to handle things.

After the birthday she had barely gotten back to her job when an urgent call came from Mr. Brown. The child had come over in tears saying her mother was asleep on the bathroom floor and wouldn't wake up. Mrs. Brown had gone over and returned to call an ambulance; Mimi was at their house but would Belle please come for her as soon as possible.

The prolonged divorce battle had taken its toll on Dixie who thought an over-dose of sleeping pills was the way out.

Belle signed her daughter into a Mental Health facility to recuperate from the nervous breakdown but was in a quandary as to what she was going to do with her five-year-old granddaughter. She couldn't take her to the resort in New Port Richey. Jeff couldn't take her: the court wouldn't allow it. Finally somebody came up with the name of a boarding school run by Benedictine nuns in a small town thirty miles north of Lakeland. A phone call did the trick and after a frantic week of buying and marking clothes she drove her little granddaughter to Holy Name Academy in San Antonio, Florida.

Holy Name Academy

The main building at Holy Name Academy (HNA) had once been a tourist hotel and had been moved a dozen blocks by teams of oxen to sit facing Highway 52 with its back to Lake Jovita (also called Clear Lake). Its three stories in the form of a T, with a full-length attic for trunks and luggage topped by the bell tower added by the nuns, looked pleasant enough the day Belle turned in the front drive.

Most of the first floor was administrative and Belle was shown to the spacious screened porch along the front where tourists once rocked in high-backed chairs. There were still chairs for waiting visitors, but she found she had to share the porch with the secretary-sister's flock of free-ranging parakeets. Belle was astounded to see the birds flying around the porch and into the open office, sitting on the top of the nun's veil or riding the carriage of her typewriter nibbling the edge of the letter in progress!

The sisters gave Belle a tour of the installations. The second floor was the convent itself: off-limits to anyone but the nuns. Two dorms for students, one for the youngest children and another for older girls, were on the third floor and Belle was taken to see where Mimi would stay. Long rows of beds ran down each side of the dorms, each with a night stand on one side and a small wooden locker for clothes on the other. White curtains on rods suspended from the high ceilings allowed each bed to be divided off into its own cubicle for privacy while dressing and undressing. However, the sister explained, the students always slept with the curtains pulled open. Each dorm had a bathroom area with a row of washbowls on one side, toilet cubicles on the other, and, to the back, several separate little rooms each with a bathtub. Also, each dorm had a separate room for the nun who served as house-mother.

Belle wasn't happy about leaving such a small child with those serious-faced women dressed all in black, but apparently they had very kind hearts.

When she went back a week later on her way to New Port Richey Mimi took her out to the front of the grounds and solemnly pointed out the life-sized statue of St. Michael Archangel in full armor that guarded the entrance. She told her grandmother that Sister Matilda Anne had informed her that since she and the angel shared the same name, he would always look out for her in a special way: he would always stand guard over her so she never need feel afraid.

Since the school had agreed to take her early because of the crisis situation, Mimi had been mostly by herself for a full week and had apparently made use of the time before the other students arrived to investigate every bit of the building, all the way up to the bell tower. She happily described how the bell in the tower was rung from the second floor by a rope that ran down from the attic through a pipe on the third floor; and how if you listened carefully when the nun downstairs began to pull several times to set the heavy bell in motion, you could hear the rope move against the sides of the pipe even before the bell started to ring.

A Missing Doll

But it was not easy for Belle to visit the school. Although San Antonio was only seventy miles from New Port Richey, visitors were only allowed on Sundays, and weekends were the busiest time for the tourist hotel. Lakeland was almost double the distance, too far to go and return in one day, and she had to use a lot of her precious leave time to visit her daughter in the Mental Health facility, make sure the house was okay, and pay bills. So it was more than a month before she could get back to see Mimi. It was an important visit.

Most of Mimi's belongs had stayed behind in Lakeland when she went to HNA: Phoebe, her toys, books, records and record player, and, outside of a traveling outfit or two, even her clothes since she would be wearing a uniform now. But the nuns had encouraged Belle to send a few favorite items - a toy, ornament or book with the child. Mimi had chosen her little red horse, her book about the little train and the "cuddly doll" she slept with every night: a stuffed plush doll with a plastic face that looked like a sleeping child in pink overall PJ's, eyes closed and mouth slightly smiling, a couple of strands of yarn hair escaping from the hood of the sleeper.

She was soft and comforting.

Apparently, the first day of school had seemed a bit scary, so when the older girls got on the bus to travel the half mile to the parochial school in San Antonio, Mimi had taken her cuddly doll downstairs and out to the little building next to the convent that housed the kindergarten. It seems the day had gone well, filled with the things kindergarten children do: crayons, paper and yarn, rounds and games, a mid-morning snack, learning to form in line, and standing or sitting when told. But at the end of the day, as the children got in line to walk back to the main building, Sister Dorothy had spied the doll under Mimi's arm. *"Oh, we don't take the toys out of the kindergarten house. They have to stay here. You can come and play with her tomorrow."* When Mimi protested that it was <u>her</u> doll, in her kindest voice the nun only replied she could come back and play with it everyday! And into the big toy box went the doll.

Sister Matilda Anne hadn't really understood when Mimi complained that a nun had taken her doll. She thought it had been lost or misplaced, but she knew the loss was significant and immediately wrote Belle about the problem. So on this trip Belle was bringing another cuddly doll, not quite the same, because this one was blue, but it made life better for Mimi.

In October Dixie was well enough for a weekend pass, so she rode up with Belle for the Halloween party at the school. Belle was bringing a gypsy costume she had promised Mimi, as well as the a pilgrim costume that had been requested for a Thanksgiving play. But the trip apparently was more stressful than foreseen and so weekend passes were put on hold for the next few of months while Dixie recuperated.

But Belle made it to the Thanksgiving play because it seemed so important to her granddaughter. That was the weekend she learned about her granddaughter's disappearances.

The nuns at HNA adhered to the idea that children should be carefully watched over and kept constantly busy. But her home situation had allowed Mimi a great deal of unsupervised time, and now and then she apparently just felt she'd had enough "structure." So, as she now confided to her grandmother, sometimes she'd just take herself off to the orange grove along the west side of the convent, choose a tree three or four rows in, climb up and settle back against the trunk to think her own thoughts for a hour or so before returning. Yes, she could hear the nuns calling frantically but they never thought to look up in the trees.

Belle was alarmed and made her to promise not to wander off any more into the orange groves, threatening to tell the nuns about her hiding place if she heard about it again.

Mimi might have wanted some time to herself occasionally, but Holy Name Academy was a haven of structure and security for all the boarding students. Belle had worried about the type of school-mates her granddaughter would have, but HNA was definitely not a school for wayward children or social misfits.

Many of the girls were the daughters of parents in diplomatic service or working abroad in situations that were felt to be inappropriate or unsafe for their children. Others, like Mimi, were temporarily without a parent to take care of them.

Were any of the boarding students homesick or unhappy at Holy Name? Undoubtedly. To the point of running away? Well, Mimi did admit that now and then that first year she would look out the little window to the right of her bed and dream up elaborate plans of sliding down the rain pipe beside it to a roof on the first floor, then down a small tree to the ground, and then across the grounds, past the statue of St. Michael Archangel and on to the highway, hoping to get back to Lakeland - or somewhere.

But she never did. In fact, there was no need to: the school had no walls or fences at all. The front "gate" was just the statue of St. Michael beside the paved entrance for cars. This was officially the limit for all students unless they were going somewhere in a group accompanied by an assigned older girl or a nun.

Belle had been informed of the school's strict policy regarding run-aways: any girl who ran away was immediately shipped off to where-ever her parents had designated on the registration form. She was gone without ever speaking to another student: the nuns packed up her things and sent them after her. So few girls ever tried to run because, like Mimi, they knew they really had no other place to go.

Angels

On one visit Mimi took her grandmother to see the convent chapel on the first floor close to the dining hall. It looked a bit odd to Belle's non-Catholic eyes but it had a "church" feel and seemed a place her granddaughter found very comforting.

The students shared in the nun's evening prayers, occupying the six pews along the outside wall while the nuns sat in pairs down the middle of the chapel and against the inside wall leaving two aisles the length of the room. Each nun had her own chair and a kneeling bench with a shelf for her prayer and meditation books. In the middle at the back the small organ on its raised platform allowed the musician a clear view of the altar. In front of the all-white altar were two life-sized angels - one dressed in red and the other in blue - kneeling with their backs against the left and right walls with the altar rail between them. Each angel held a glass lamp where a short, fat candle flickered permanently.

Mimi was so enthralled with those angels that Belle went out and bought her a little angel statue for her night stand. It was special in that all day it absorbed light from the window so that it could glow softly all night as she slept.

DIVINITY CANDY

2 ⅓ cups granulated sugar
⅔ cup white corn syrup
½ cup water
¼ teaspoon salt
2 egg whites
1 cup chopped nuts
½ teaspoon vanilla flavoring
one or two drops of food coloring as desired

Stir first 4 ingredients together in saucepan over low heat until sugar is dissolved. Boil, without stirring, until a small ball of mixture forms a hard, almost brittle ball when dropped in cold water (265° F. on candy thermometer). (Sugar crystals that form on sides of pan should be removed with wet cheesecloth wrapped around tines of a fork to avoid falling back into the mixture and causing crystallization.) Remove syrup from heat; slowly pour over stiffly beaten egg white while beating by hand or with electric beater until mixture loses its gloss and a small amount, dropped from spoon, holds it shape. Add nuts, food coloring and vanilla; pour into greased 9" x 9" x 2" pan. Cool; cut into squares. Makes about 1 ½ pounds.

from Belle's kitchen

A difficult year

Christmas that year was celebrated, but not joyfully. On the way to Lakeland Belle picked up her granddaughter at the beginning of the school holiday. She tried to inject some Christmas spirit into the house by making Divinity Candy, asking Mimi to help by picking the nut pieces out of the shells. Jeff came up from Bartow on Christmas day and Mrs. Montgomery, one of Belle's best friends came to share Christmas dinner.

But it was a somber occasion as Dixie wasn't well enough to leave the Mental Health facility and the worries over her frail mental state cast a shadow over the holiday. The house seemed haunted by so much past unhappiness that Belle was glad to head back to New Port Richey after the New Year and even Mimi seemed to look forward to seeing all her friends back at school.

Every month that second semester Belle visited the school, and at each visit she gained insights into boarding school life as Mimi chattered away about everyday things: Sister Matilda Anne walking through the dorms each morning ringing a little hand bell to let the students know it was time to get up; the uniforms and how to take care of them; how to polish black and white saddle shoes without getting black on the white and white on the black; what the students did during Saturday play time; about the hikes they took out to the dairy farm owned by the convent; how they got to wear slacks under their uniform skirts when it was cold which meant they could stop being lady-like in their skirts and hang upside down from the monkey bars and do other things usually reserved for boys!

Cracker Cowboys

Eventually it was time for summer vacation. Dixie was scheduled for a series of weekend passes to get used to living at home again, so Belle looked for a job in Lakeland. She had always been there for her family in the past and figured she was never more needed than now. It was surprising how quickly the skills learned at the resort got her a position as secretary for the Lakeland office of the Girl Scouts of America.

Plans were made to celebrate Mimi's sixth birthday with a party at Eagle Lake, near Bartow, where Jeff had a house on the north side of the lake. Toward the south end of the lake there was a pavilion open to the public with a bath house, changing rooms, and a quick-food counter with a very limited selection.

The party was to be held there on the picnic tables under the trees a short distance from the long wooden pier jutting out into the lake. Several yards beyond the pier was a large wooden platform floating on steel drums for people who knew how to swim well enough to get there, while the children could paddle in the shallow water and play along the nice little white sand beach.

The party was fun. A group of girls Mimi's age came with their mothers, but the trip itself turned out to be the highlight of the day because the little caravan of cars encountered one of the last groups of real Florida cowboys.

Only a few years before there had been a state-wide outcry when the legislature tried to pass a law forcing cattle owners to fence their pastures to keep cows off the roads. There were more and more cars every day and with the increase in the number of cars had come an increase in the number of encounters between cows seeking warmth at night on the black-top roads and motorists with deficient headlights. The ranchers fought long and hard to block the law and continued to free-range their cattle and hold roundups in the style of the old West.

Except that in Florida cattle were not herded with lassos which were useless in the shoulder-high palmetto. Instead they were frightened out of the palmetto by cracking ten to twelve-foot whips and then moved along with the help of dogs. That's how the old-time native Floridians got the nickname of "Crackers."

Eventually the state legislature did manage to pass a law, not mandating fences, but making the owner of any cow hit on the road liable not only for the loss of the animal but also for the damages to the car. Then fences went up. But not before that day in August when the party group encountered a sizeable bunch of cattle being herded along the Eagle Lake road by four or five scraggly cowboys, mounted on typical Florida small, rugged cow ponies and accompanied by a half-dozen motley hounds.

Across the highway they went, whooping and cracking their whips in fine style!

Lakeland Again

By the end of the summer Dixie was home, at least temporarily, and Belle was settling into her new job in Lakeland at the Girl Scouts of America office. However, in consideration for Dixie's continued frail mental health, Belle made the decision to board Mimi at Holy Name Academy for another year.

This was first grade, which meant getting on the bus to ride the half mile from the convent to St. Anthony's, a small parochial school in a very small town, where large rooms held two classes each under one teacher. There, Sister Theresa, the convent secretary Belle had met on her initial visit, was also first and second grade teacher. Sister Theresa was distinguished for her special knack for teaching the Palmer Method that produced beautiful script: the kind of handwriting nuns are famous for.

Mimi was excited and chattered the whole trip to San Antonio about the friends she looked forward to seeing and how she was finally going to go to real school.

Because Dixie was still in recovery Belle remained as contact person for HNA, and that was a very good decision. As the year progressed it seemed that she was always getting phone calls from the school about one problem after another.

First, in October, there was the accident at recess. Recess at any school is a highly prized part in the school day: play time! St. Anthony School fronted on the town's large central park. An the side nearest the school were two large sets of swings, five or six seesaws, a slide and plenty of open area under big oak trees for games of tag. Those oak trees were the cause of the accident: they had long protruding roots that ran out over the ground before burying themselves in the sandy soil.

From what Belle heard, at some point while playing, an older student had accidentally bumped into her granddaughter causing her to fall and hit her head hard on one of those roots. Mimi was only out for a few seconds and, after sitting down a bit, said she felt fine as the students went back in to class. But in the time before lunch she put her head down on her desk and went to sleep. She got on the bus at noon like a sleepwalker and returned to the convent. But when she started vomiting, lunch was out of the question and she was taken to the nun's infirmary while a doctor was called from neighboring Dade City since there were none in San Antonio. Mild concussion; two days in bed. Nothing much to worry about.

Then in December, the school had a bout of measles, and the child barely got over them in time to come home for the Christmas holiday.

But not all was bad news and problems: Dixie was finally better. She was home permanently and looking for work. The divorce had been settled and Dixie had been allotted a judgement for alimony which would allow her to live comfortable. But she and Belle agreed that having something to do would be helpful, even though, now that the divorce was final, Dixie seemed much less stressed, especially now that she was in counseling with a local Catholic priest.

But then came June! Just a few days before the beginning of summer vacation the state of Florida decided to vaccinate all school children against smallpox. Although the disease was almost eradicated in the United States at the time, the health authorities were still keeping their guard up.

Unfortunately no one knew Mimi was coming down with chicken pox at the time and the smallpox vaccine got into the chicken pox pustules and spread to cover her whole body - even in her hair and inside her mouth!

An urgent phone call summoned Belle to come pick her granddaughter up immediately! Once home, the house was quarantined for almost three months with only the attending physician allowed to enter and leave. Although friends could stand at a safe distance outside the windows and talk to those inside, groceries and supplies had to be left on the porch to be taken in once the delivery person had gone.

For six weeks in the middle of Florida's hot, hot, summer Mimi thrashed with fever in her mother's bedroom darkened by closed blinds to prevent light damage to her eyes, while both Belle and Dixie worked to keep her from scratching the sores that itched so terribly. They were trying to prevent permanent damage since scratching the scabs off would have left big scars. Each time they changed her, every scab had to be softened with warm water so none were pulled off with the night gown, otherwise more scarring. There was no birthday party that year but the whole family celebrated the fact the child had survived.

Actually, Mimi's seventh birthday was celebrated with a special ceremony. Belle was aware that the nuns at HNA had impressed Dixie during her mental health crisis, and that as a result she had contacted the Catholic priest at a church in Lakeland. Belle thought it had been for counseling but then it turned out Dixie was taking baptismal classes and had scheduled her baptism together with Mimi's on that birthday in 1952.

Dixie also argued convincingly to have Mimi at home for the next school year, enrolling her in St. Joseph's parish school in Lakeland, instead of Holy Name Academy. A plan was worked out. Dixie had found a job in the evenings at a drive-in theater. That meant she could take her daughter to school in the morning and pick her up in the afternoon before leaving for work. And Belle's daytime job at the Girl Scout office let her be home in the evenings. Dixie's position didn't seem like much of a job to Belle, but it was undemanding and their schedules worked out well.

Since they also got free passes, Belle often drove out with her granddaughter to spend the evening with Dixie at the drive-in. These were all the rage at the time: with cars increasingly affordable and television not really popular yet, a drive-in provided family-fun at a reasonable price. The whole family (or a group of friends) could enjoy a movie and pay only the one small entrance fee for the car. The film was projected on a huge outdoor screen and viewed from the car parked next to a post holding a speaker on an extension cord that allowed it to be hooked over a partially-raised window. Each drive-in had a concession stand for hot dogs, french fries, popcorn and such. It was a great place to spend an evening, but Belle and Mimi must have seen *The Quiet Man* and *Singing in the Rain* at least six times each!

Mimi seemed OK with the arrangement, even though she complained about missing her friends from HNA. She also missed Phoebe who had died several months earlier while she was away at school. Belle found her a little dog which, of course, was immediately named Lassie, and for her birthday Dixie bought her a pair of tiny turtles that lived in a special little dish. The turtles lasted, but Lassie either ran away or got "dognapped."

That year the drive in, Mimi's school and Belle's office were closed for over a week in early October when Tropical Storm Hazel, almost but not quite a hurricane, roared through. As usual there was a flurry of last-minute preparations: food to be bought and cooked, the bath tub filled with water, flashlights, candles, kerosene lamps and sterno burner brought out, and all movable items stored in the garage so they wouldn't blow away.

As the storm moved over the house it blew just right to turn the chimney into a sort of musical instrument, producing a very low penetrating sound that evoked thoughts of goblins, ghosts and banshees. Hour after hour the moaning went on until everyone's nerves were thoroughly frayed!

The storm drains couldn't handle all the rain and the whole neighborhood was under almost a foot of water.

Fortunately the house was built on a slight rise and they weathered the storm with no problem other than having to splash their way to the mail box for a week while the water subsided.

Mountain Vacation

As soon as school was out after second grade the family took off for a summer trip. Dixie was so much better that she wanted to go somewhere - anywhere. She loved to drive and Belle wanted to see the beautiful Smoky and Blue Ridge Mountains, so a leisurely route was mapped out all the way to the Green Mountains in Vermont. Coming from flat western Illinois and even flatter Florida, Belle found it exciting to be able to stand high up in the mountains and see all the countryside around.

North Vermont has some lofty peaks, but in the southern part of the state these mountains are more like a high, wide, upland plain or plateau. The family stayed near the Green Mountain National Forest at a bed-and-breakfast farm that sat at the foot of a low rounded mountain where a busy stream of icy cold water hurried downhill over granite boulders. The rivers and streams in Florida are mostly slow and lazy: despite starting in a rush of clear cold water from numerous deep springs, they quickly become warmed by the sun and tinted the color of weak tea by the tannin in the leaves that fall from overhanging oaks. So this busy little "wannabe" river was a source of constant amazement for Mimi who explored every rock and tiny waterfall.

The trip took them all the way up above Dorset, Vermont, stopping at a quarry to see how marble is pulled from the mountain to be cut, polished and finished. Everyone bought pieces to take home as souvenirs or future presents. Belle bought a lovely little what-not box with a lid for her dresser, and a solid cube of beautiful green and black veined marble as a paperweight for her desk at the office. Dixie picked up an ashtray, and Mimi, always horse crazy, chose a square black marble paperweight because of the horse head engraved on it.

After Vermont they headed straight west to Cleveland to visit a priest Dixie had been corresponding with since becoming a Catholic. Although their conversation wasn't long, he impressed Belle as being a kind-hearted person and certainly seemed to have been a good influence on her daughter.

There had been little sightseeing between Vermont and Cleveland but now they turned south to Cumberland Falls Park. All three enjoyed the park, the river, and the falls, but none so much as Mimi: this was Daniel Boone country but also Davy Crockett country and as they drove through the forest and along the river, Mimi imagined herself in a scene from the movie *Davy Crockett King of the Wild Frontier*. Her joy was complete when, with a solid riverbed and low water level, Belle took her to wade across the river just above the lip of the falls! Through the park they went and then turned north to visit relatives in Oak Park and Barrington near Chicago for a week or so before returning to Florida.

As soon as they were home, Belle got out Mimi's uniform skirts to see how much the hems would have to be let down for the coming school year. Mimi took one look at the St. Joseph uniform and suddenly announced that she wanted to return to Holy Name Academy!

No arguments could move her. Not even the prospect of having to give up the two turtles that were supposed to lessen the loss of Phoebe could make her change her mind. Mimi had been very faithful in taking care of them, but of course they couldn't go to HNA with her. So she decided they could live free like the rest of the turtles in Florida, took them to neighboring Lake Bonny and turned them loose.

San Antonio

Since Dixie's divorce had become final, she now had some extra money from back alimony as well as the title free and clear to the Lakeland house. Her job as a ticket taker at the drive-in was not at all fulfilling and suddenly Lakeland seemed to hold little to offer: during her health crisis most of her friends had moved away or moved on. Now with her new-found Catholic faith, San Antonio began to look attractive.

San Antonio was a very small town but with easy access to good education. Moreover, it was a Catholic town, founded and developed in the late 1800´s to provide a safe haven for Catholic families facing discrimination in other parts of the country.

Belle could see the attraction of a safe, wholesome environment to raise a daughter, but she was sure Dixie would soon get bored and become dissatisfied living in such an extremely small community. In any case the decision was made to move to San Antonio and enter Mimi as a day student at St. Anthony's - not, perhaps, what the child had in mind when she said she wanted to return to Holy Name Academy.

Belle decided to stay in Lakeland: she had reliable transportation having traded the car Jeff had given her for a good upgrade. And she liked the independence her job at the Girl Scouts office gave her. Since nothing was owing on the house, the agreement was that Belle would continue to live there rent free, paying only the upkeep, utilities and taxes. Dixie didn't even want to take any of the furnishings, saying they reminded her too much of Jeff since he had chosen and bought everything without even consulting her.

Dixie rented a house in San Antonio - Belle thought it sorely rundown - and began to form relationships in town.

But Dixie hadn't really investigated the reality of employment in the area, just upped and moved! It turned out just about everything in San Antonio revolved around family owned and operated agribusiness: orange groves, chicken farms and cattle. And apparently there weren't even any jobs available for her limited skills in the nearest larger town, Dade City, some six miles to the east. Eventually she found a part-time job posting accounting information for a company in Tampa. Even though the company was on the side of Tampa closest to San Antonio, it was still a dangerous drive of almost an hour each way several times a week over a narrow, bumpy black-top road that tended to flood in heavy rains.

Belle was used to small towns; she had spent all those years out on the farm and then lived happily in little Frostproof, Florida. But her experience in Chicago and even Lakeland now made San Antonio seem too small. There really wasn't much to the place at all: fewer than 300 people in town. State highway 52 curved around south to avoid the town itself and crossed the major thoroughfare, Curley Street, three blocks south of the central park. That was where the town's gas station stood. Four blocks north of the park, on the same Curley Street, the town ended at the railroad tracks and tiny train station where trains didn't stop but where mail was picked up (snatched off a hook) and sent out (thrown through the open door of the mail car as the train rumbled through). So the town itself was only about five blocks wide by seven blocks long with each house set separately on very ample lots.

And there wasn't much in those few blocks that comprised downtown San Antonio itself. There was a small hotel with some few permanent residents and fewer tourists; a very small bar which no woman ever dared approach; and a general store next to a small house that tried and tried to be a business: first a beauty salon that just didn't take off, then an antique store targeting tourists who never came, then a "hamburger hangout" for teens that had little money and less interest, and finally a Tea Room nobody visited!

There was no business section: no drug store, no soda fountain, no movie house, no clothing nor shoe stores, no health center nor doctor. The general store was fairly well stocked and had a small vegetable section and a cold case for fresh meat, but for anything that couldn't be had there, the residents had to drive the six miles to Dade City or thirty miles to Tampa.

On one corner of the central park was a tiny building with the Post Office and a Credit Union lumped together. Since there was no home mail delivery, the town's residents came in regularly to share town news as they got the mail from their assigned boxes. Across the street a small building housed the Volunteer Fire Department's one tanker, and the sheriff's one holding cell. The school and St. Anthony Catholic Church took up the entire length of one side of the central park and the other three sides were residential. And that was it.

With such a lack of things to do or places to go, for the longest time the only real hang-out for the town´s children was the reduced-size baseball diamond in the central park. However, at some point the town had decided that young people needed something more than baseball to keep them from getting into trouble. So the three blocks down to Lake Jovita were paved and a tiny pavilion with a couple of tables and benches built beside the small patch of white sand hauled in for a beach. With the installation of a boat launching ramp on one side, entertainment in San Antonio was complete.

Water Hazard

Belle wasn't keen on swimming: the farm had offered no opportunity to learn. And she knew her granddaughter had no notion whatever of how to swim but was fearless around water: Mimi had almost drowned in that same lake the first year at boarding school when she went down the slide into deep water and had to be rescued by an older student. The freedom the small town afforded and the closeness of the lake made Belle very uneasy.

To Belle's mind, the lake was dangerous, not only because of the possibility of drowning, but also because in summer the recurrent polio epidemics that swept across the south seemed to be somehow related to water recreation.

It had really started the summer Dixie was born, 1916, when an epidemic of infantile paralysis, Poliomyelitis, swept through the US. Every year after, one part or another of the country suffered summer outbreaks; the 1940's and 1950's were especially bad. Since no one really knew how the infection spread, public events and swimming pools were closed and families fled the affected area. In fact, a polio outbreak in Florida in 1947 had been was one of the reasons they had traveled north that summer.

Children seemed especially susceptible to the disease and so many died each year. But even more horrifying was the possibility parents faced of seeing their child creep through life on crutches with braces on withered legs or, worse, confined for life in an iron lung, quadriplegic and unable to breathe on their own. So many hospitals had wards with row upon row of iron lungs! In summer every bout of fever was cause for grave concern.

The country was working hard to conquer polio. President Franklin D. Roosevelt had founded the *March of Dimes*, a national campaign that raised private money for polio research. Year after year a darling heart-breaking poster child in leg braces reached out to Americans asking them to fill cards with dimes for research. And year after year people filled those cards, and prayed they and their children would be spared.

With wonderment Belle heard the news right after Easter in 1954 that the students of St. Anthony school were to be part of a nation-wide vaccine field trial for polio. All the students in the school, along with thousands more in other parts of the country, were to be vaccinated in a study where some towns received the vaccine while others received a placebo, each not knowing which they had received.

The results, published in 1955, showed the vaccine was highly effective and it was approved for general use. However, since nobody knew if the San Antonio students had received the vaccine or the placebo, all were eventually re-vaccinated.

But at last Belle didn't have to worry about Mimi getting polio when she played at the lake. Now if she would only learn to swim!

Bells

Belle drove up to San Antonio for Christmas that year and it was a special experience for her: for the first time she really heard the bells in San Antonio.

The convent's one bell marked the work day for the town, ringing at 6 a.m. and 6 p.m., but also at noon for a special Catholic ceremony where everyone stopped to pray for a minute, even parking by the side of the road to get out of their cars and stand in prayer.

Belle knew that would never work in a city!

Mimi said that sometimes the bell rang in a different way and then you were supposed to count the strokes, because that bell meant one of the nuns had died and tolled once for every year, not of calendar life but of convent life. Everyone in town knew all the sisters and many were related to them, so families with relatives in the convent nervously counted the strokes until eventually the bell told them who had gone to heaven. Then the town would begin to gather at the convent to say good-by before the sister was taken for burial in St. Leo Abbey's cemetery.

But Christmas was different. Neighboring St. Leo Abbey also had bells - many bells, fancier bells: bells that sounded much like a carillon - and for Christmas the Abbey used them all. Dixie had arranged for the three of them to go to midnight Mass at the Abbey and, as they parked the car along the highway and started up the long walk to the church, the bells playing Christmas carols rang through the quiet, cold night filling the silent orange groves and pastures with joy.

All through Mass the bells played, and for an hour after the carols continued as they sat over a cup of hot chocolate before going to bed for a while until Christmas day dawned. It was beautiful and moving - much nicer than the recorded music the downtown stores played in Lakeland!

Yes, Christmas was special that year and, despite the run-down house and tiny town, Belle enjoyed it. Dixie was in good spirits and Mimi was elated counting the presents under the tree. From Belle, Dixie had learned the joy of shopping for just the right gift for each person, and both of them enjoyed seeing the carefully wrapped and decorated packages fill the space under the tree.

As much as Dixie liked giving presents, she especially liked receiving them, so Belle always made sure there was something special for her in Mimi's name as well as her own. Jeff never came to San Antonio but always sent a gift, usually clothing, for his daughter. And Belle's relatives in Illinois always sent a box full of presents from each of her siblings and their families, so the decorative skirt under the tree was full.

But this Christmas Belle brought some disturbing news with her: Jeff's Monday-through-Friday girl, now common-law wife, was dead. During a pre-Christmas celebration at the house on Eagle Lake she apparently developed an acute reaction to a combination of cold remedy and the alcohol in her drinks, and went into shock. Eagle Lake was thirty minutes from Bartow over a road much worse than the one to Lakeland and she was dead on arrival at the hospital.

Belle's heart ached for the pain of the little eight-year-old girl out at Eagle Lake whose mother was suddenly rushed one evening from the house and never again seen alive. But the topic was a very sore spot with Dixie so Belle never mentioned the girl to her again, and never, ever, to Mimi.

Easter Chicks

The following Easter, Dixie and Mimi drove to Lakeland to spend a few days there. Belle thoroughly loved the Easter season traditions and had decorated baskets, bought chocolate rabbits, and, of course, hidden colored Easter eggs around the house for her granddaughter to find. Through the house the child went, searching under and behind the furniture, carefully placing each egg in her little basket.

But then for some reason she took an old sweater and bundled it into some sort of "hen" shape, stuck in a few turkey-bird feathers found in the back yard and placed two colored eggs under it, announcing that in twenty-nine days they would hatch! Of course those eggs were hard-boiled! Of course her "hen" wouldn't incubate anything!

Where on earth did the child get that idea? Belle felt little Mimi must have paid very close attention to all the stories she had told about her childhood on the farm, or else, how would she know the correct incubating time for chickens?

The "hen" and her eggs went back with Mimi to San Antonio, safely carried in a cardboard box ¨nest¨ lined with pine needles, and the countdown to that special twenty-ninth day was on. Poor Dixie! When the day came she had to drive all the way to Dade City and buy two baby chicks to replace the eggs before her daughter got home from school. And, of course, then they had to arrange warmth for the chicks, food, water, etc., etc., etc. San Antonio permitted keeping a reasonable number of chickens in the back yard and those two chicks were the start of a nice little flock of hens that eventually produced plenty of eggs for the little family with some left over to sell. Belle was happy to see her granddaughter's new interest in chickens because the little flock on the farm, especially the darling baby chicks, had been one of the greatest joys of her childhood.

New Job, New House

Through that whole first year in San Antonio Dixie continued to commute to her job in Tampa and Belle could see that job would soon become a problem, since during summer vacation Mimi would be home every day with no one to care for her. Belle certainly couldn't take time off from her job to baby sit for three months.

The solution came unexpectedly. Sister Theresa called Dixie in one afternoon and said, "*Ms. Gentry, I don't want an answer now, but if you would consider teaching office science at the high school here, please come back another afternoon and we'll talk about it.*" Belle guessed Sister knew Dixie's first inclination would be to say no!

But Dixie thought about it and went back and talked, and the upshot was she agreed to teach typing and shorthand at Holy Name Academy high school for the 1954-1955 school year. Although a few years before the divorce she had finally managed to get her undergraduate degree from Florida Southern College, she had a lot of work ahead of her during the summer months finding appropriate materials and brushing up on her office skills, especially shorthand.

Dixie also surprised Belle with the news she had bought a house! All during that year while renting, she had looked around town for a place to buy and now, with a good job guaranteed, finally found one set on the north end of a large piece of land that fronted on Curley Street. The lot was deep and wide enough to split into three smallish house lots, except that the south end tended to get boggy where a stream from the pond in back had once run down to Lake Jovita. But the middle portion was okay, as was the north end where the small two-story house sat with a rundown little barn /garage and a utility shed in back.

The original idea, Dixie informed her, was to sell off the two unused lots, but it seems no one was interested. And the problem with having so much land was having to mow it. Mowing was a big chore in the days when even a power mower was a luxury and personal riding mowers unheard of. Fortunately the neighbor that owned the grove to the north and west offered to run his big tractor-mower over the south lots every time he did his grove, and the man that mowed the right of way did the same. And when it came time to spray the groves, a short detour was made to include the four orange and two grapefruit trees that separated the house lot from the rest of the land. Nice people in San Antonio!

But the house was set really close up beside the north boundary line. Should anyone decide to build on that side, the two houses would be a bit too close for comfort.

The structure itself had originally been a tobacco factory with one big work room downstairs under an upstairs loft for drying the leaf. Entrance was by a porch in front and shipments went out from a large loading dock in back. Year after year tobacco dust accumulated in all the cracks and corners of the entire structure so now there would never be a need to fumigate: bugs just couldn't live there. When the building was converted to a house, the back loading dock was closed in for a kitchen, and that kitchen was horrible: no counters, just a cold-water faucet over a tiny sink set on a two-by-four frame, along with a filthy stove! And the floor had a definite downward slope away from the main house.

At some point an inadequate indoors bathroom had been sectioned off from the kitchen; it was as bad or worse than the kitchen it came from! The bathroom floor was also sloped and the door was positioned right in front of the toilet in a direct line with the front door. The cracked washbowl was, like the sink, set on a wooden frame, only this frame was showing clear signs of rot. Dark and dingy, it looked as if it hadn't been cleaned in years.

The main work room downstairs had been partially divided in half leaving a large archway between the two halves. The front half had been made into a bedroom on the right and a tiny open sitting room on the left, while the back half was left as a long living-dining-whatever room. Upstairs were two bedrooms where the ceilings sloped down to within thirty inches of the floor. At some point in time, a tiny closet had been partitioned off in a corner of each room.

All the floors were rough pine planks and most of the walls were narrow tongue and groove boards. Someone in the past had tried to improve the looks of the place by hanging wallpaper. But that had obviously been a very long time ago. Over the years the paper had split along the grooves and the paste had weakened, so the rooms were now festooned with limp strips of much faded wallpaper. The former owner of the house was an elderly person whose family no longer lived in the area and was uninterested in the house or its contents. They sold the place "as is" when their relative died. "As is" meant it was absolutely full of stuff: old dirt, old papers, old furniture, old left-over junk!

All in all, the house was a super-fixer-upper. Belle herself had lived in a place like that when she and Monta first moved to Florida. The memory gave her the shivers and made her wonder what on earth had possessed her daughter to invest in such a junk pile. It was going to take a lot of work and money to make that house livable!

Yes, it was a fixer-upper. And that's what Dixie and Mimi did for the next five years. The heavy work was contracted out, but mother and daughter did all the finishing work, although they had to learn as they went. Often workers hired for some job that required heavy labor or special skills would take the time to show them how to do the finishing work themselves.

The very first item before moving in was renovating the bathroom which involved placing huge jacks under the beams of the original loading dock area and bringing it level with the rest of the house. Once leveled, that door that opened into the main room was eliminated and a sliding door was installed to open off a very small hall space gained from the bathroom area. No longer was the toilet in direct view from the front door!

The next time she came to visit Belle was astounded to find the dark, dingy, unappealing bathroom transformed with rose-colored fixtures and tile, set off by walls papered in a pale pink and cream flowered pattern. It turned out that the next door neighbor was a retired master tiler who had been glad to do the job at his own pace and a much reduced cost.

Belle was in agreement with her daughter: the kitchen was most definitely next on the list. Since it had been leveled along with the bathroom, it was ready for new linoleum floor tile. Spacious pine pantries, and new counters with a back-splash tiled to the hanging cupboards were installed. Together with a double sink and drop-in stove they made a wonderful work area on the long axis of the kitchen "L" while on the short axis a small table with two chairs under the north window formed a breakfast nook that looked out over blue hydrangeas. The only problem was the counter and cabinets were crafted to Dixie's 5'7" height, so in order to put some dishes away Belle, barely 5'2", and Mimi, even shorter, had to use a small step-stool!

Every year something else was done, usually during summer vacation when Dixie and Mimi could help with the work. All the walls in the house were covered with sheet rock (dry wall), and hard-wood floors with basketball court finish for easy care were laid over the original boards.

Since the rooms downstairs were open to each other, they were all painted in the same light warm-grayish sand color. All, that is, except for the downstairs bedroom where Dixie hung wallpaper in a springtime-inspired print of small yellow flowers on an off-white background. It gave the whole room a soft glow that reminded Belle of the yellow tied-comforter of her childhood. That comforter had been her mother's and with time the chintz had mellowed into cloud-softness. All through her childhood years Belle had so loved to snuggle herself to sleep in soft yellow joy. How heartbroken she had been the day the material gave out and suddenly began to split in so many places that the comforter had to be thrown out! Emma had made her a new one but, of course, it was never the same.

This room gave Belle that same feeling of being enveloped once again in her beloved yellow comforter.

Dixie had taken so much care with every detail. Besides the main door, the room had another smaller door that led to a side entrance to the main house so whenever there was company in the front sitting room whoever used the bedroom didn't have to walk through a conversation to get to the rest of the house. But there were windows in the other two walls, so this was the only place for a chest of drawers, and with that little door at one end and the closet at the other, there was only so much space available. Dixie had scoured both Lakeland and Tampa looking for a piece that would fit, but with no success. Finally she convinced a furniture manufacturer to make one to the exact specifications. That, and matching twin beds under the front windows and a small night stand finished out the decor. Belle found it gratifyingly comfortable, since on her previous visits she´d had to make do with a folding bed set up in the middle of a very drab, depressing room.

The tiny front room became a formal "parlor" with a small, ornate love-seat, matching chair, and one tiny round table. Monta's prized bookcase and, eventually, a piano filled out the limited space.

Even though Florida escapes the frigid winters of the north, there are definitely cold and colder spells. Originally the only heat in the house came from an old oil burner installed in the big open central room that never managed to put out enough heat to that area or any of the other rooms. From the beginning, plans were made for central heating and air conditioning, with ducts and registers installed as work progressed. As soon as all the downstairs had new dry wall, the oil heater was removed even though the upstairs was as yet unfinished and had no heating vents. But that old heater hadn't ever done any good up there, anyway.

Eventually the upstairs rooms were also re-done. In each room the little window on the south side under the ceiling slope was eliminated to allow for an ample closet with folding doors. Although there were hard-wood floors downstairs, the staircase was so steep that Dixie was afraid someone would take a tumble and thought carpeting would help cushion a fall, so the stairs and both bedrooms were carpeted.

Dixie painted her front room in a color called *New Silver* that at times looked sort of pale green and at other times seemed gray, depending on the light. She also bought new furniture.

Mimi's room in back opened to the west so it was painted in Wedgewood Blue to cut down on the light and give it a feeling of coolness. White furniture was bought unpainted from the Sears catalogue and finished at home. Matching curtains and bedspread in a flower print, also ordered from Sears, finished out the decor. When Dixie announced the rooms were ready, Belle carefully made the trip up those steep stairs to see the result: both rooms turned out to be very attractive and very comfortable, despite the low eaves.

The main downstairs room was obviously both a living room and the dining room. But it wasn't comfortable to sit in - even less so to watch television there. So towards the end of the renovations Dixie decided to built a sun room or "Florida room" on the back with access both to the main room, the kitchen, and the back yard. The sun room had windows all around the south and west sides so the wood-paneled walls were stained a soft ash-brown to cut down on excess light. Belle especially liked the bright tropical-print cafe curtains that Dixie sewed to make it possible to watch television during the day. Rattan furniture ordered from a store in Tampa perfectly finished out the tropical look. It was Belle's favorite room of all and she spent many hours there.

Five years of planning, building, nailing, sanding and painting, looking for the right paint color, and searching for affordable furniture and decorations for each room: it was a lot of work but it seemed to Belle that the project had given her daughter a purpose in life and taught both her and Mimi a great many skills.

When the house was finished, it was comfortable, light and airy, easy to take care of, and definitely elegant in an understated way. Belle thought it much nicer even than the house in Lakeland. Her daughter had really surprised her.

Waterproofing

There wasn't much to do in San Antonio during the months of summer vacation until the Pasco County School Board made the decision to join with the Red Cross to offer swimming classes to all the children in the county. The idea was to not only "waterproof" the children, that is, lower the number of drownings in a lake-filled area, but also keep them out of mischief.

The School Board loaned its buses to the program and routes were scheduled through all the small towns and hamlets in the county to take the kids to Lake Iola for classes because, although it was quite a ride, that lake had proper changing rooms, a lunch counter, several docks, and a nice beach. The Red Cross provided the instructors and life guards.

For a dime a day, children could catch the bus in the town square and have a whole morning of instruction; for another five cents they would be picked up again in the afternoon for just fun! So even while work was being done on the house, Mimi was learning good swimming skills.

And Belle could finally stop worrying about the San Antonio lake pavilion.

Worry

But Belle didn't stop worrying about her granddaughter The strain of teaching seemed to wear Dixie down and the child was bearing the brunt of it all. The first signs had been during a visit at Easter. For some unfathomable reason, on Good Friday Dixie became enraged over nothing, shouted at both of them, then stormed upstairs, locked the door of her room, and refused to come out. Saturday went by and no amount of calling or cajoling got so much as an answer. Easter Sunday was more of the same. When Dixie missed Mass and refused to come out for lunch, Belle was forced to make a decision: she had to be at work on Monday morning and needed to start back to Lakeland. And she had no idea how long Dixie would stay in her room since school was on holiday for the whole next week. She didn't feel comfortable leaving her granddaughter alone to fend for herself for what could be a whole week, so she had Mimi pack a few things and took her back to Lakeland.

Of course, she couldn't leave the child home alone in Lakeland either, so out of necessity Mimi spent her days working on a hastily bought coloring book, stringing chains of paper clips, and walking down the flight of stairs to the *Hole in the Wall*, a tiny donut shop right next door. Late Friday morning Dixie showed up as if nothing had happened - no explanation, no apology - just picked up her daughter at the office, leaving Belle to bring the clothes left behind at the Lakeland house on her next visit. It was worrisome.

Unfortunately that wasn't the only occasion. The next Christmas Dixie pulled the same stunt again and pretty well ruined Christmas for all of them even though Belle tried to distract her granddaughter by teaching her how to make the special fruit gelatin dessert they always had for Christmas. As they worked,

BELLE'S CHRISTMAS GELATIN

2 regular or 1 large pack raspberry gelatin
4 sweet oranges, peeled so no white inner skin remains, with the
   pulp pulled out and section skins discarded (so as not to give
   a bitter taste to the dessert). If no really sweet oranges are
   available, the oranges must be prepared a day ahead and set
   in the refrigerator with 2 tablespoons of sugar.
1 fresh peeled pineapple cut into pieces and cooked for 5 minutes
   with three tablespoons of sugar or one can pineapple tidbits.
20 large, sweet grapes, halved and with seeds removed
2 large bananas, sliced thin

Prepare the fruit separately. Prepare the gelatin according to
package instructions and set aside to cool a bit.

Mix the fruit in a large mold or casserole and cover with the
cooled, but not set, gelatin.

Refrigerate until fully set.
Serve with a topping of whipped cream.

from Belle´s kitchen

Belle worried: was Dixie headed for another breakdown? Was she going to make Belle take Mimi back to Lakeland again? However, this time her daughter reappeared after a week, just before Belle had to leave.

Finally Belle figured it out. One night as she fretted, tossing and turning in bed, she had heard Dixie come down the stairs shortly after midnight and realized they no longer needed to worry so much about her: when she shut herself up in her room she had a supply of sandwiches, a thermos-full of coffee, a carton of cigarettes, and a couple of romantic novels, and just wanted to vegetate for a few days. This was her daughter's way of having some needed quiet time. Of course, Dixie was taking advantage of Belle's presence to look after Mimi and was careful not to outstay Belle's visit again.

But this explanation didn't convince the child, nor did it make up for one ruined holiday after another. There should have been a better way to handle this but Belle couldn't think of one. Her resources were limited: she couldn't take more time off from her job; she certainly couldn't take Mimi to her father, and in any case the child wanted to be with her mother: wanted to celebrate with her mother, open Christmas presents or fix Easter baskets with her mother.

There was nothing Belle could do but try to be there for her granddaughter as best she could.

It was on her Thanksgiving visit that Belle heard from Mimi about her attempt to run away to Lakeland. It seems Dixie had whipped her severely for such a minor thing as chewing two pieces of gum in one afternoon! So, Mimi said, she took off through the groves and side trails heading for Lakeland, feeling sure she had memorized the route traveled by car so many times. She figured all she had to do was walk the four miles down Highway 52 to the back road that led around Dade City and directly to Highway 98 before it got dark, and there she'd be able to hitchhike to Lakeland. She had enough money for a local call to her grandmother to come and pick her up wherever the ride left her off: big schemes for a little girl. She had actually made it all the way past the convent almost to St. Leo when a wide swampy creek running down to Lake Jovita forced her to leave the groves and cross the creek on the highway. That's where the highway patrol was waiting for her. Belle worried about Dixie's reaction but Mimi said everything had been all right, her mother had just come out to the street as she got out of the patrol car and never mentioned the incident at all.

On the Back Steps

Sitting on the back steps Belle watched the chickens greedily peck at the special mash she'd set out for them. As a small child her older sisters had taught her the secret of happy chickens that produced big eggs with perky yokes that stood up brightly in the frying pan: four overflowing cups of bran to one package of dry yeast or one half inch square of wet yeast, together with a tablespoon of sugar and enough warm water to wet the whole thing down. Left to rise for an hour or so at the back of the stove, the very aroma brought the hens running.

Twice a week she mixed up a batch for her granddaughter's little flock of Rhode Island Reds that had developed from those two original Easter-egg chicks. The warm mash made the hens cluck and sing, and Belle so enjoyed the sound of happy chickens that every afternoon with decent weather found her sitting with Phoebe's replacement, a large tiger tomcat, in her lap either on the warm back steps or on a log in the shade of the big grapefruit tree.

Retirement hadn't been as bad as Belle had feared and she wondered if she should have stayed on at the office that last year and a half after the first warning heart attack. Her job hadn't been too strenuous and she had really enjoyed working for Girl Scouts of America. She might had stayed on except for the stairs: the office occupied the back half of the second floor of an older building downtown. Originally one huge open space, it had been divided into two almost-equal areas.

The front half had a small cubby-hole bathroom which left more than ample space for her desk and filing cabinets, plus a waiting area for visitors. Her boss' office and large conference/planning table took up most of the back half with another small bathroom and a tiny storage closet at one end. Unfortunately, the only windows were in the back wall.

Because she had to work all day in artificial light Belle had made a special point of using her lunch hour to get out in the sunlight. Occasionally she would walk the three blocks to Morrison's Cafeteria to meet a friend for lunch, but most days she brought a sandwich from home and hurriedly ate it at her desk so she would have time to stroll around to the nearby stores.

It wasn't that she wanted to buy anything; her closet was full since every year she bought herself a new outfit, alternating years between winter and summer outfits. And she took very good care of her clothes by using the nice cotton dresses Dixie always gave her for Christmas around the house. No, she certainly didn´t need more clothes, but just liked to window shop and, since over the years she had come to know most of the long-time employees in those stores, she would sometimes stick her head in to say hello to a special friend here and there.

Belle felt she had quite a nice group of friends, even though the number wasn´t large. Although some wondered if living by herself might be lonely, she didn´t feel that way at all. For one thing, she enjoyed quiet moments; they gave her time to think.

But during the week her days were full at the office where

the phone rang and people came and went constantly. The weekends were full, too. Saturdays were for grocery shopping, catching up on house work, and maybe a cup of coffee with Mrs. Brown next door. Sundays she usually chose to meet friends after church for a leisurely lunch, or she would go over for a visit with Mrs. Montgomery or drive out on the Bartow road to see the Raulersons.

That left only the evenings free and, since she disliked driving at night, Belle usually spent them at home in the company of the big radio Jeff had bought for the house: *Jack Benny, Amos 'n' Andy, Dragnet*, and music shows filled her evenings along with the <u>Saturday Evening Post</u> that took her a whole week to read cover to cover. Belle had spent endless hours reading to Mimi from that magazine during the years they lived together in Lakeland and she still carefully cut out and saved the *Watchbird* cartoons for her granddaughter.

Yes, Belle enjoyed her independence, and enjoyed her job. But those stairs were a problem. She'd known these many years that her heart was not in good shape: in fact, ever since she'd almost died when Dixie was born. Well, in spite of her heart she'd had managed to stay employed well past retirement age until that second attack make it obvious to everyone it was time for her to quit.

And here she was living with her daughter and granddaughter.

At first she had been leery of leaving the independence of Lakeland and moving to San Antonio. She greatly disliked her daughter's periods of isolation and feared her sudden outbursts of rage. But after her arrival everything with the family seemed to get better.

Yes, things were definitely better. The house in San Antonio was finally finished, and when she decided to leave Lakeland, the house and furnishings there, except for her few personal belongings, had been sold. She even sold her car since she wouldn't be driving much anymore and it just cost too much to keep up.

The sale of the house provided enough money for her daughter to pay off any remaining bills from the renovation in San Antonio, put a generous down payment on a better car and still let the family take a long, leisurely summer vacation.

Westward Ho!

Belle's stories of Yellowstone Park had sparked her daughter's imagination and this trip Dixie wanted to explore the western part of the country. The decision was made: westward they would go! The trip was carefully planned all through the winter months with the help of new Rand McNally maps that not only showed the roads, but also gave detailed information on driving conditions, millage between cities, gas stations, places to stay, special sites to visit, scenic pull-offs, etc.

At Belle's request the family decided to drive north through Chicago and then take a northern route west, returning by a more southerly route. Off they went: first to Chicago to see all the relatives in Oak Park and Barrington; then on to East Moline to visit more relatives; and finally over to Rossie, Iowa, to see cousins her granddaughter had never met - three brothers and their families.

These cousins were serious farmers who worked what had been their parents´ original farm plus large lots of neighboring rented acreage counted in quarter-mile squares. That part of Iowa is divided in grids by alternating paved and unpaved roads each half mile. That year just one of the families had planted sixteen quarter-mile sections!

When they inherited the farm, two of the brothers bought out the third's share and that brother in turn invested the money in heavy farm machinery he then rented out, first to the family and then to others. But they all worked the acreage cooperatively, splitting income after expenses, which included paying each other the cost of machinery rental and the use of the land. The arrangement provided a good life for all three families.

When Belle and the girls got there everyone - absolutely everyone - was busy harvesting oats prior to planting corn. There were lots of children Mimi's age and there were always small jobs for the kids while the men did the heavy work and the women kept up a running conversation while cooking an endless succession of meals. But four days were long enough to catch up on all the family news and these people were really, really, busy so on the threesome went.

Since this was a "nature" trip, they took lots of secondary roads to avoid all large towns, concentrating instead on the unfolding scenery of plains, forests and mountains with streams and fantastically beautiful waterfalls. They ate picnic lunches at extravagantly scenic pull-offs, and stopped at every something-to-see that caught their fancy.

From Iowa their route took them to Chamberlain, South Dakota, to visit one of the charities Dixie contributed to regularly: a school for Native American children on the Lower Brule River below Ft. Thompson. Then they turned west through what is known as the Badlands where they searched for dinosaur fossils, then through the Black Hills, stopping at battlegrounds, learning Native American lore and US history.

Finally they arrived at Cody, Wyoming, their base for the much anticipated visit to Yellowstone National Park. Old Faithful Inn was still there and seemed to Belle to have been much improved. Although the original rustic look had mostly been preserved, everything else had been updated. There was even indoor plumbing for everyone:

no more outhouses for the staff!

They bought souvenirs at the lodge where Belle retold her bear story; toured the geysers, paint pots, and hot springs; visited the falls and lake; and finally left Cody to cross the park heading for Butte, Montana, with its stark open-pit mines.

What a depressing landscape, Belle thought. It was a relief to leave the area and travel through mountains and Lolo National Forest to beautiful Lake Cour d'Alene in Idaho. They enjoyed the lake for a couple of days before continuing westward into Washington State by way of Spokane, skirting around Seattle for a brief visit to Vancouver, Canada, where Belle repeatedly exclaimed over the splendor of the flowers in the city's many gardens. Florida with its super-hot summers could never produce such beauty as the mildly cool, moist climate of Vancouver.

Turning south and avoiding major cities, they worked their way down through Oregon into California all the way to Mt. Whitney and the Sequoia National Park to see the giant trees. Along the way a side trip was made to see the Pacific Ocean. This was the first time Belle had seen the Pacific and, since she was used to the ultra-white sand beaches and calm water of Florida's Gulf coast, the wild, cold water and rocky beach they visited didn't impress her very much.

On south they went, traveling between parks to Bishop, California, where they finally turned east for the trip home: Tonopah, and then across the desert to Ely, Nevada, and south to avoid Denver. Suddenly tired of traveling, they picked up the pace, hurrying along secondary roads, through Pueblo to Wichita, across the Mississippi River at Memphis then through south Tennessee, foregoing every tourist attraction to scramble down off Eagle Pass heading for Atlanta and then home. It had been a glorious summer!

The next improvement in family life was Dixie's decision to get a Master's Degree in Business Education. Belle could see that Dixie liked teaching and had come to realize that she would need a higher degree if she ever wanted to get a job in the area outside Holy Name Academy. She was pleased her daughter was finally making serious plans for the future.

With Belle in the house Dixie could now stop dreaming and start studying.

So Dixie began attending summer sessions at the University of Florida in Gainesville. This meant she was gone for about two months each summer. Since she stayed in almost-deserted dorms, this time away from home gave her the rest and quiet she needed to recuperate from the demands of family and job: no need now to shut herself up in her bedroom as she had done so often before. Every year Dixie came home in a good mood, refreshed and feeling like she was actually getting somewhere in life. It made living with her so much easier!

While she was gone there were just the two of them at home, and Belle helped her granddaughter as much as she could to "turn out" the house: cleaning down to the last corner, even taking down the venetian blinds to be hosed clean on the clothes line outside. And the whole time together they talked. And talked. Belle told her granddaughter stories about her growing-up years: about Puppy and the cows; about the Indians at the back door, opening her jewelry box to show the little flintnapped stone arrowhead found at the buffalo wallow so many years ago.

Belle got her prized quilts down from the upper shelf of the closet and shared their history, starting with the blue and white Ohio Star pieced by Monta's mother the year before she died. Nancy (Snell Gist) hadn't been able to finish the quilt so Belle had joined the pieced blocks together and her sister-in-law Pearl had done the quilting: thus three of the four corners had a name and date embroidered.

That design had been very popular at the time and the second quilt was a multi-colored Ohio Star. This was true patchwork with each star composed of different materials set in pink "paths". Belle lingered over it, fingering each block, remembering the person whose dress or shirt had contributed the material. Pearl's mother, Emily Warner, had pieced it in 1928 and years later industrious Pearl had done the quilting and given it to Belle so it, too, had names and dates embroidered on the corners.

Mimi noticed that the third quilt, a showy flower basket patchwork and applique design, had no names or dates and asked why. Because, Belle told her, it had been bought from a cottage craft store on a trip she'd taken with 'Deal through Appalachia and the person who made the quilt hadn't "signed" it, probably thinking only family heirlooms merited identifying the maker.

Finally Belle got the box with the four thistle-design wine glasses from the back of her closet, told the story 'Deal had shared with her so many years ago, and gave them to her granddaughter.

Major

The family circle suddenly included a horse! Like most young girls, Mimi was horse crazy and for once Jeff and Dixie agreed on something and decided to buy her a horse for her birthday. Holy Name Academy said they could keep it free of charge in their now-unused pasture and stables which made upkeep feasible, so the search was on and eventually they were referred to a family outside Dade City. The daughter who owned the horse was ready to leave for college and wanted to sell her much-loved gelding before she left. But she insisted on personally interviewing each prospective client to make sure he went to exactly the right owner.

Major was a slightly aging roan Tennessee Walker. Familiar with horses from her farm days, Belle knew that meant he had five beautiful gaits, including the famous Tennessee "walk" that covers large stretches of ground effortlessly. So Belle, Dixie and a very excited Mimi made the trip to Dade City to be inspected: Mimi passed the inspection because apparently Major really liked small girls and let them boss him around endlessly. But, oh my, thought Belle, he was so very big - 17 ½ hands high - and Mimi was still so small! She looked like a bauble perched up on top of a mountain of horseflesh.

Besides being a pushover for small girls, it turned out that Major was a huge fan of home made pie. He liked Belle's apple pie but made a special slobbery mess over the hand that fed him pieces of her cherry pie, so Belle found herself making them just to please the big lug!

A Secret Revealed

The month she was to graduate from eighth grade Mimi came home one afternoon in tears. Belle knew that eighth grade graduation - a formal ceremony in red cap and gown - was a big deal for her granddaughter since it meant leaving St. Anthony school that only offered primary grades to study at the convent high school. But it wasn't until that afternoon she found out just how much the child had wanted her father present at this ceremony.

As the tears slowed the whole story came out.

Mimi hadn't wanted to call her father from the phone in the kitchen and risk everyone in the house and on the party line overhearing her conversation, so she had taken a handful of coins to the public phone booth on the corner down by the general store. She gave the operator her father's office number. He wasn't in. Because it was a person-to-person call, the operator asked for another number where he could be reached and someone in the office gave the house number. The female voice that answered at that number said, no, Jeff Gentry wasn't home. When the operator asked to whom she was speaking, the voice answered, *"This is his daughter."*

Shocked, Mimi had just hung up. The tears started on the way home as she realized how many secrets her mother and Belle had hidden from her all these years.

Now she was full of questions: questions that Belle decided to answer, but not in front of Dixie. They had to wait until she left for Gainesville so they could talk freely. Then the whole story, or at least a censored part of the whole story, had to be told.

Yes, she had a sister: a sister that looked very much

like her, a sister just a year younger than herself. They had never told her because the girl's mother had felt uncomfortable in the presence of a reminder of Jeff's first family and demanded the girls be raised separately. Although the mother had died several years earlier, that's the way things had continued on.

After that, before each scheduled bi-yearly visit to her father, Mimi would phone ahead and ask for her sister to come along. There was always an excuse: a school field trip was scheduled; she was off visiting a relative in another town; she wasn't feeling well. After a couple of years Mimi got the idea. She decided to take matters one step further. The summer she turned fifteen she phoned her father to announce that she was coming to spend a week and "get to know him." What was the poor man to do? He couldn't get rid of his other daughter for that long and so the two girls finally got to meet.

Mimi came home excited and full of news. Their rooms were painted and decorated just alike - same color, same bedspread and curtains. They had the same taste in clothes and had separately chosen the same outfit to wear to a hop at the Civic Center where they looked so much alike that in the half-light people mistook her for her sister! (Now the true story of the in-fashion, well-fitting clothes that arrived every Christmas came out: Jeff took one daughter shopping and then bought a second, identical outfit for the other.)

Mimi was enthralled to have a sister, especially a sister her own age, a sister that was like her in so many ways but with new friends and new activities. Since under current Florida law one could get a learner's permit at fourteen and a full driver's license at sixteen, Mimi now asked for, and got, the car for frequent weekend visits to Bartow. After all, weekends at home were either reserved for grading papers or full couch-potato times of rest from work. With church and store within walking distance the car wasn't much needed, and early on Belle had warned her daughter that if Mimi wasn't allowed the car she would catch a ride to Dade City and go by Greyhound.

They agreed the car was safer.

Yes, Belle noted, the two sisters were very much alike and yet very different. Jeff kept a jealous eye on his younger daughter, always suspicious that she was up to some mischief. As a result she was often rebellious and frequently untruthful. Mimi had been raised with more trust and the freedom a small town afforded, and she had been taught to respect that trust. As a result she obeyed curfews and told the truth about where she was going: if she hadn't, in that small town the truth would have been known from a dozen sources within twenty-four hours. Her half-sister was considered "wild" by her classmates but Belle knew nobody would have ever applied that description to Mimi.

But the two sisters learned from each other: in the two years they had together before Mimi went off to college her sister learned how to get more leeway from her father by being less obviously rebellious and more communicative. But, it was a good thing that special college-oriented summer schools took up most of Mimi's free time during those two years, because in their short time together her sister taught her to dance the twist, smoke cigarettes without coughing, and drink 7&7 (Seagrams 7 with 7-Up). Belle suspected but never asked.

Retirement

No, life in San Antonio wasn't bad at all: television was a wonderful invention - much better than radio - and with the others out of the house most of the day Belle had plenty of time to keep up with the numerous soap operas that brought vicarious life to the sun room. In the morning before the programs began she'd walk the few steps up the street to visit with Mrs. Evans, the next-door neighbor originally from Wales who always seemed to know all the latest news in town: Belle suspected she spent a lot of time listening in on the party line. And of course, in the afternoon she'd take a little nap and then have her time with the chickens before starting supper.

In fact, getting supper ready was the only work she did in the house, because sorting and running clothes through the washing machine couldn't be considered work. Her granddaughter even saw to the drying on the line outside. At first Belle had wanted to do the ironing but soon found out that Mimi really enjoyed that task, so now she limited herself to sprinkling down the clothes on Saturday morning so she could sit and talk as roll after damp roll disappeared from the basket and the neat piles of ironed clothes grew.

Dixie took care of everything outside: the yard, the car, and the grocery shopping. And Mimi took care of the inside: dusting, vacuuming, cleaning bathrooms, windows and floors. So Belle took on the cooking, making sure supper was ready right at six. All in all she thought this a good arrangement since she really liked to cook and it was obvious her family relished the food she put on the table.

She also taught her granddaughter to cook, passing down some of her cherished family recipes, like the one for turkey stuffing. Being from the North, Belle had never taken to the Southern custom of using corn bread for her stuffing. She wanted white bread, even if she had to bake it herself! Also, even though she could made do with store-bought sausage patties, she sorely missed the bulk sausage they used to put up on the farm: the first run of sausage was packed into casings and smoked but, as the weather turned cold, the last of the sausage was always left in bulk which made it much easier to fix dressing.

BELLES SAUSAGE STUFFING

1 pound spicy (hot) patty sausage
2 quarts lightly packed bread crumbs
1 cup finely minced onion
1 cup diced celery
2 tablespoons minced celery leaves
½ teaspoon celery seed
½ teaspoon salt (or to taste)
¼ teaspoon pepper
½ to 1 cup hot water to mix
1 or 2 tablespoons sage if you like savory stuffing

Make bread crumbs from oven-dried bread by placing in
a plastic or paper bag and rolling with a rolling pin (or run
through a grinder on coarse cut).

Break up the sausage meat with fingers in a large bowl or
container. Add all the other ingredients except the hot water
and crumble between fingers until the sausage is well mixed
with the bread crumbs. Add in hot water slowly just until the
mixture clumps together slightly in the hand - do not add too
much water.

This receipt makes enough to stuff an
8 to 10 lb. turkey.

from Belle's kitchen

119

The one thing she really did miss after leaving Lakeland was going to church. Everything in San Antonio centered around the Catholic church on the square. True, there was a small white-painted Methodist mission chapel several blocks away that now and again had a student-preacher come in, but she was Presbyterian, not Methodist, and in any case that chapel was too far away for her to walk and her daughter certainly wasn't going to drive her there! Of course, there were some church programs on Sunday morning TV and she often tuned in, but just hearing a sermon wasn't the same as actually being in church.

Belle enjoyed good preaching and loved to sing the Psalms and hymns, but never really understood what was going on in the Catholic service: never quite knew when to stand up and when to kneel down and couldn't understand the Latin words. So she only went on special occasions like Christmas midnight mass at St. Leo Abbey to hear those beautiful bells, and sometimes the Easter service in town when the church was fragrance with lilies.

In any case, church or no church, Belle had a deep, personal, trusting faith in God and knew who she was in His eyes. Only one small formality was pending which she planned on taking care of as soon as she could. She felt quite content with her place in creation as she sat on the back steps enveloped in a sense of peace and well-being, contemplating the simple beauty of clouds and breeze, trees, grass and happy chickens.

Adventure in Central America

San Salvador was delightful! During the day the air was so soft and warm she could almost pat it. At night the breeze came in fresh from the surrounding mountains where house lights on the hillsides twinkled like stars. It felt so much like spring, but every morning dozens of women came walking down from mountain farms with masses of bright poinsettias in their arms to sell in the streets reminding all that this was Christmas, Central American style.

Sunshine and flowers were not much like the snow she'd left behind in Oak Park, Illinois, less than a week ago. Despite the weather, it had been okay living in that big old house with her nieces these last four months.

(Nieces! The word made them sound like a generation apart, but like most of her nieces and nephews they were a bit older than their aunt: that's what comes of being the baby of a large family.)

Belle had taken the train north with her daughter and granddaughter. After settling Mimi in for her first semester at college in Ohio, she and Dixie had continued on to Oak Park where she had stayed while Dixie flew back to Florida to store the furniture and things, rent out the house in

San Antonio, and leave for a teaching job with the State Department-run American School in El Salvador.

Yes, that trip to Illinois had been okay, but even though she was used to traveling by train it had seemed overly long and tiring. However she had insisted on the train: despite Dixie's experience as a pilot, airplanes never seemed safe to Belle! Of course, a train to Central America was impossible, so it was either stay the whole year in Oak Park with her nieces Marion and Gail, or go out to O'Hare and get on a plane for the first time in her life.

Mimi had been assigned to accompany her and had come prepared for anything and everything, from tranquilizers to under-the-tongue nitroglycerine tablets - just in case! But once in the air it had been so entertaining to sit in a comfortable seat and watch the earth unroll - just like a movie - as the plane slowly gained altitude. And then there was the fascination of seeing the topside of all those clouds. So fast, too! In less than one day they had come all the way from Chicago's snow and ice to this warm, green tropical country. Why, she'd never, ever, take a train again!

Yes, Casa Clark in San Salvador was a long way from Oak Park. Who'd ever thought she'd travel so far at her age; after all, she was seventy-five!

Oh, but she was enjoying this adventure! It was so nice here: nice weather, nice boarding house, and very nice people. In the evening there were a number of English-speaking permanent boarders who gathered for dinner and conversation. Of course, during the day they were all at work, but the battalion of little Indian-faced maids that worked here were all so friendly: they talked away at her non-stop while they dusted and swept and cleaned. No matter they didn't understand English, nor that Belle had never learned even one word of Spanish; she smiled and nodded as they chattered away and brought endless glasses of juice or small plates of fresh papaya and pineapple to the rocking chair in the wide corridor where she sat watching the humming birds busy with the flowers in the sun-filled patio.

Endings

Belle hadn't wanted to accompany her daughter abroad during the next school year. El Salvador had been wonderful but Midway Island out beyond Hawaii in the Pacific Ocean seemed just too far away. Neither had she wanted to spend another cold winter in Oak Park, but rather opted for a nice rocking chair on the screened porch of the hotel/boarding house on the corner of Curley Street and Michigan in San Antonio, less than a block from their former house and close enough to visit with Mrs. Evans.

The company had been nice enough there and Mimi had come down for a quiet Christmas - very quiet compared to the fireworks and piñatas they enjoyed last year in San Salvador! San Antonio had no public transportation of any sort so without a car they just visited and had Christmas dinner with the other elderly guests.

Well, that school year on Midway Island had come to an end and Dixie seemed to have finally worked out the restless spirit in her. She'd taken a teaching position at the Community College in Fort Pierce, Florida, over on the Atlantic coast, and found a house to rent near the college. She´d already arranged for the furniture to be sent from the storage facility when she drove up to help Belle pack.

It was a rather long drive, first over to I-95 then down the coast to Ft. Pierce, so it was late afternoon when they arrived. But Belle wanted to see the house before going to the motel where Dixie had been staying while signing her contract at the college and looking for a place to live, and eventually doing some preliminary house cleaning.

Well, Belle thought the house unimpressive. Part of a new neighborhood, it was quite small and inexpensively built in the modern boxy, cookie-cutter style builders were turning out by the thousands. But it was new, so new that there was no grass in the yard: the only landscaping on the lot were two baby scrub oaks and a palm tree planed in sand and still supported by wooden braces. New meant probably clean; it would do for the two of them.

Perhaps a bit of painting and more plants would help give it character, but that could wait. Fortunately it came with curtain rods already installed and Dixie had bought inexpensive ready-made curtains at Sears plus a ladder to hang them with.

After an early breakfast at the diner near the motel, they took the two beach chairs and metal ladder Dixie had bought and drove over to the house so Belle could sit and watch as her daughter hung curtains on all the important windows. They had barely finished the lunch picked up at the supermarket delicatessen and served on paper plates when the movers arrived. Belle took her chair off to the entrance of the kitchen where she would be out of the way and let Dixie have a free hand in directing the movers so all the heavy pieces of furniture wound up in the proper place.

Dixie had sold some furniture when she moved but kept the rattan sofa and chairs from the Florida room; they looked right in place in the living room of this house. As did the dining table that had rarely been used since they preferred eating off TV tables while watching their favorite programs.

All the boxes were numbered and labled so those with kitchen items were set along the little bar that separated the dining area from the kitchen, while the rest went into the third bedroom until they could be unpacked at leisure.

There was no furniture for that bedroom: when viewing the house in San Antonio the family that eventually rented it had fallen in love with Mimi´s room and bought the furniture as it was. Dixie sold it without hesitation, even including the drapes and bedspread. She felt sure Mimi would have out grown that type of decor by the time she finished college.

For now, this room was a perfect place to sort out things and once that was done she would buy some adult furniture for that room before the Christmas holiday.

By the end of the day the curtains were hung and the beds made up. With familiar furniture in place, and the kitchen pretty well organized, they had a place to live: no more motel. iBelle was already looking foreward to having a kitchen of her own again!

Dixie celebrated by taking Belle to dinner in downtown Ft. Pierce at a restaurant that fronted on the inlet right where it met the Indian River.

In a very short time the house began to look like a home and Belle was just beginning to feel settled in when suddenly a blinding headache hit.

Belle woke up in a hospital bed with no memory of fainting but still with a horrible headache. Only now her eyes wouldn't focus properly and when she tried to talk her mouth felt sluggish and the words came out all slurred. Worse, her right arm and leg wouldn't move at all!

All she could do was to drift in and out of pain-filled sleep.

Calls were made:

> *"Your grandmother just had a stroke and the doctors are not at all optimistic. It looks like you'd better come on home as quickly as you can so you can say good-bye. I've already talked to the college office and you have permission to leave right away.*
>
> *There's a ticket waiting for you at the airline counter for the afternoon flight to West Palm Beach. I'll pick you up there."*

Things happened in a murky haze: sometimes it seemed as if Dixie were with her but once Belle even thought Mimi was talking to her. That was just plain silly: her granddaughter was so far away at college in the north!

> *"Grammie, Grammie, can you open your eyes and look at me? I've come home to see you!"*

Yes, it really was her granddaughter! Now if she could just get the words out everything could be fixed up right!

As a child on the farm, Belle's family had attended a church that only baptized adults when they made a public personal decision for Christ. She had moved to Chicago before that happened and, although she had attended a church there, that church presumed all adults had been baptized as infants and so the question never came up. The same had happened in the churches she attended in Bartow and Lakeland.

Belle had always intended to be baptized, but it was just one of those things that seemed to slip by day after day.

And now she had run out of days!

Slowly, one mumbled word at a time, she asked her granddaughter for help.

But the next day Mimi came with upsetting news.

"???"

"I'm sorry, Grammie. This hospital doesn't have a chaplain. I don´t know this town very well but I called six or seven different churches from the phone book and couldn't find anyone willing to come.

The Presbyterian minister asked if you were a member of his church or if you had a letter from your former church. The Catholic priest won't baptize you until you take special classes, and the Baptist minister said OK but wants to wait until you get out of the hospital since they only baptize by immersion... Oh, I'm so, so, sorry!"

"!!!"

"Yes, I realize how important it is but I just don't know who else to turn to!"

Somebody must have been willing to come, because through the haze of semi-coma Belle felt water dribbling on her head and face as she heard the familiar sacramental words.

Now things were right; now she could let go and drift with no fears and no doubts!

Did Belle realize it was her granddaughter who had dared to borrow a basin from the nursing station and tearfully performed the rite of baptism?

Probably not, she never regained consciousness and died peacefully two days later on September 26, 1965.

www.ingramcontent.com/pod-product-compliance
Lightning Source LLC
Chambersburg PA
CBHW030532020726
47494CB00004B/1333